Liberating Mrs. McTavish

Captive Western Widows

Cheryl Wright

Copyright

Liberating Mrs. McTavish

(Captive Western Widows)

Copyright ©2024 by Cheryl Wright

Small Town Romance Publications

Editing: Sarah Lamb Editing

ALL RIGHTS RESERVED

Dedication

To Margaret Tanner, my very dear friend and fellow author, for her enduring encouragement and friendship.

To Alan, my husband of over forty-nine years, who has been a relentless supporter of my writing and dreams for many years.

To You, my wonderful readers, who encourage me to continue writing these stories. It is such a joy knowing so many of you enjoy reading my stories as much as I love writing them for you.

Table of Contents

Chapter One

Karisvale, Montana – 1880s

From the very moment Donald McTavish set eyes on her, he told Mary she would be his wife. Laughing his words aside, never did she believe he would pursue her as relentlessly as he did.

Donald was a force to be reckoned with, and eventually she'd given in. Almost immediately, Mary had regretted accepting his proposal of marriage.

Mary wasn't thrilled with Donald's plan of marrying at the courthouse, but she had no choice. Donald didn't want a church wedding—instead he wanted a quiet wedding away from prying eyes. It meant Mary was unable to invite her family and friends. In fact, he'd demanded no one was told about their pending marriage. At least not until after the event.

The entire scenario bothered Mary more than she dared admit. The pair hadn't known each other long, a matter of weeks at most.

There were no words of congratulations as they made their way out of the courthouse, no well-wishers, and certainly no rice thrown over the happy couple.

Within moments of the pair stepping onto the courtroom steps, instead of the peacefulness she anticipated filling her heart, Mary heard gunshots—three in quick succession.

Mary's elation turned to fear, and her heart pounded. Turning to her groom did nothing to appease her, as his arm slipped away from hers.

Donald McTavish lay dead on the ground—with three bullets to the chest.

His new wife had no choice but to rush inside to what she hoped would be safety. Why anyone would kill her husband, Mary didn't know. Her mind was full of scenarios, but it also left her wondering what she would do now.

Sheriff Henry Walters appeared long after the shooters would have been well gone. In his own defense, he stated he'd inspected her husband's body, and had it transported to the morgue. He'd interviewed witnesses, all of whom denied seeing the shooting or those responsible.

Mary felt as though she was living a nightmare. She'd become a widow within minutes of marrying her groom. Her mind was in turmoil and she didn't know what to think. Or what to do. "What…what happened?" she asked in a voice she didn't recognize as her own. "Why would anyone want to kill my Donald?"

Sheriff Walters sat opposite Mary, studying her for what seemed forever. "I can't give you an answer, Mrs. McTavish," he said.

Mary was convinced the sheriff knew more than he was letting on. She stared down at her clasped hands. They were white from her clenched fists, and stood out against her pale blue wedding dress. The dress which was now covered in her dead husband's blood.

Henry Walters stood to leave, but stopped momentarily. "My advice to you, Mrs. McTavish," he said sternly, "is to leave town immediately. As his wife, you inherit everything Donald McTavish owned, including his home. If it were me, I wouldn't worry about such things during this difficult time."

Her face felt tight, and her head was pounding. Had she married a murderer? Or some equally unsavory person? "I…" Confusion engulfed her, and Mary's head spun.

"You do know what your husband did for a living?" he asked.

They'd known each other such a short time, it was not something Mary had thought to ask. She shook her head briefly. Now she wished she had waited, given herself more time to get to know her now dead husband.

"Your husband was corrupt in the worst possible way, Mrs. McTavish," he said, leaving Mary shocked. "Get out of town and don't look back. Under no circumstances should you wait around to see what happens next." The sheriff spun around and left the room, leaving Mary more confused than ever.

She stared at the sheriff's retreating back until she forced herself out of the fearful trance she found herself in. Mary hurried to the front of the courthouse and glanced out the window from behind the dark curtains. People hurried along the boardwalk toward their destination.

Had they heard the news? Were they the ones to see what happened, yet refused to say so? It made Mary all the more determined to discover what Donald had been involved in. Corruption was what the sheriff told her, but in reality, it told her nothing.

She hurried out of the building and almost ran to the home she was to share with Donald. The townsfolk stared at her, and it took until she was almost home to realize her blood-covered gown was the reason.

Donald had given her a key to the house that very morning, only minutes before they were to marry. Her heart pounding, Mary glanced about. Was she to be next? Her hands shook uncontrollably.

In the end, she held one hand over the other in an effort to get the key in the door. Hurrying inside, she locked the door behind her, and ran into the bedroom she was meant to share with her new groom. He had moved all her belongings there earlier today, after telling her in no certain terms she could no longer live at the ranch she'd inherited from her parents. The thought hadn't crossed her mind, but Donald wanted her to sell it. His insistence greatly upset Mary.

Standing in the doorway of what was to be their bedroom, Mary's heart still pounded, although she felt more protected here. She opened the closet and pulled out her carpetbag. The one she was to use on her honeymoon. Their luggage had already been delivered to the train station, but Donald insisted she take an overnight bag in case of a mix-up. Upon opening it, Mary noticed the bag was already packed. Donald had been thoughtful in that way, and she appreciated it. Poor Donald. No one expected to be shot and killed on their wedding day.

Tears began to fill her eyes, but Mary fought them back. She had little time to spare—she must get out of her ruined wedding dress as quickly as possible, and clean herself up. Then she could be on her way.

But where would she go? If she was also on the killer's list to die, how could she get away without being seen? The sheriff's words reverberated in her head. *Get out of town, and don't look back.*

If that's what it took to get herself out of this mess, the mess Donald had put her in, then that's exactly what Mary intended to do. Except she couldn't afford to be recognized. She slumped onto the side of the bed. This time, tears rolled down her face. She could no longer hold them back.

Did that mean she was doomed? The last thing she wanted was to endure the same fate as Donald. Whatever he did, she was not involved.

Giving herself a few minutes of tears lifted a burden from her shoulders. Mary had to leave town, but she would leave unseen. A plan was forming in her rattled mind.

She only hoped it worked.

~*~

Standing in front of the ornate mirror, Mary pulled her hair back into a tight bun and tucked it under a decidedly male hat. It was the very hat her husband had brought to take on their honeymoon, so no one would recognize it as Donald's.

She had already removed and discarded her bloodied wedding gown and bonnet, shoving them into an unused cupboard where she hoped they wouldn't be found. Mary decided the only way out of this dilemma was to assume the identity of a man. Holding back a sob, she splashed water on her face, hoping it would clear her red and puffy eyes.

Donald wasn't a huge man, but his clothes would be too big for her. Mary did some quick mending, then shrugged into one of his coats. She hoped that would cover her up enough that no one would notice she was not a man.

Snatching up the money Donald told her was stored in the house, along with the train tickets he'd purchased for their trip, she added it all to an envelope. That was then added to the inside pocket of her husband's oversized coat. She would wait until dusk, then make her way to the train station. The train they were booked on left soon after that. She would hide on the platform until it was time to leave.

Mary wondered if her life would ever be normal again.

Chapter Two

Luke Flanagan felt sorry for Mary McTavish. She'd found herself caught up in the indiscretions of her husband. Had they planned to marry another day or two down the track, she would have been spared the grief.

He watched her hurry into Donald's home, her new home, and wondered if she would be fool enough to stay there, or would flee as the sheriff had advised. Every word spoken in that room had been heard by Luke. What he would do about Mary, he wasn't yet sure. She may not realize it, but she was deemed a witness to her husband's murder.

For that reason, she had to die.

It was a pity. Mary was a pretty little thing. He'd been watching the pair for a while now. With the criminal connections Donald had, Luke could see the writing on the wall. The man was dispensable. But what of his new wife?

He sat back on the wooden bench at the train station and checked his pocket watch. The train would be here any minute—she would have to show herself soon. The moment she did, Luke would be right behind Mary McTavish in her ridiculous outfit, pretending to be a man.

As naïve as she was, he doubted Mary would even be aware of his presence. He dressed respectfully, calmly read the newspaper while he waited, and blended into the background.

The train pulled into the station, which was suddenly filled with black smoke and squealing brakes. The smell was almost overpowering.

Crowds flowed from the train, and when it was clear to do so, new passengers boarded.

There was no sign of Mary McTavish.

Luke glanced about. He knew exactly where she was hiding—he'd seen her go into the porter's closet. There was nothing more than cleaning equipment stored there.

"All aboard!" the conductor called.

Glancing up, Luke noticed a porter hurry up the steps of the train. There was still no sign of Mary. He ran to the porter's closet, but she was no longer there.

It was then it hit him. Luke ran to the train. He barely had time to board, but the conductor was kind enough to let him pass since his new bride was already waiting on board for him. The wink he'd given the conductor was the deciding factor.

He should have known Donald would purchase tickets for the Pullman car. The man had far more illicit money than he would need to last a lifetime. He had lived the high life until his recent indiscretion. Stealing from his *client* sealed his fate. If he'd returned it, they would forgive him this one time, but never again.

Alas, Donald dug his heels in, and had to be eliminated. The fool brought it on himself.

Not that Luke was convinced they would have let him off the hook after handing the money over. If indeed money was the indiscretion.

He could never be trusted again. Besides, Rufus Hanson was not the forgiving type.

Hurrying into the lounge area of the Pullman car, he glanced about. That same porter he'd seen board the train only minutes before was heading toward the honeymoon suite. Donald really had gone all out.

Standing back, not making a move, he waited to see where Mary McTavish went. Once she was in her room, he would corner her, and she would have no means of escape. His heart pounded. She was in a tremendous amount of danger and was oblivious to the truth. If Luke knew Donald, he would have left no stone unturned to ensure that money was hidden. All he had to do was tell them where the money was. His stupidity put his pretty little bride in danger.

Luke shook his head. Why did it have to come to this? He put his hand inside his suit jacket, and assured himself his prized colt was still there should he need it, which he likely would. He played his next move over in his mind. More than anything, he knew Mary would be terrified. Would she scream upon seeing him standing in her room?

He couldn't allow it to happen. If he did, all sorts of people would come running, including the railway detective. It wouldn't be pretty. He'd likely have to kill them all, otherwise they'd kill him first.

It would land him in a mountain of trouble. Shaking the thought away, Luke reassessed the situation.

Walking at a normal pace, he headed toward Mary's room. The last thing he needed was to be noticed, so hurrying was out of the question. Besides, it gave her time to feel comfortable in her surroundings. She may not be so reactive that way.

He watched as she unlocked the door and entered the large suite Donald had purchased for their trip. Nothing had been spared—he obviously wanted to impress his new bride. His heart pounded as he took the last steps toward the suite. This was the last thing he wanted to do, but he was compelled to do it, no matter his objections.

Reaching out to open the door, a shiver went down his spine. It was now or never, and the latter wasn't an option.

His hand on the door handle, Luke turned it, but it was locked. He knocked gently on the door. "Room service," he called softly, trying not to be heard by others, but hoping and praying Mary opened the door.

"I didn't call for room service," she answered tentatively through the locked door.

Luke could hear the trepidation in her voice and didn't blame her one bit. If he'd been in her shoes, he would be worried too. "It's a gift for the newlyweds from the railway," he lied, hoping that gained him entry.

There was no answer, and Luke was certain he was going to have to force his way in. It was the last thing he wanted. He couldn't afford to make a scene and raise suspicion.

The click of the door unlocking had him sighing with relief. The door opened a crack, and the beautiful widow of Donald McTavish appeared before him.

"May I enter?" Luke asked.

She looked him up and down, grazing him from head to toe. He wasn't in a porter's uniform, and that might be to his detriment, but his suit gave him respectability.

"Of course," Mary said, then opened the door wide.

The naïve woman would have no idea what was about to happen.

Chapter Three

Mary stared at the stranger as he entered the suite. Something wasn't right, but she couldn't put her finger on it.

Even as she looked him up and down, tingles went up and down her spine. Goosebumps covered her arms. Mary knew she'd done the wrong thing giving this man entry to her private suite. That was before she noticed he had no food tray or anything else with him.

Her heart pounded and she felt lightheaded. In mere seconds, he pushed her inside, then shoved her onto the bed, but not before locking the door behind him.

Without being able to see her reflection, she was convinced she was pale. As if her situation wasn't bad enough, he opened his jacket and showed her his gun. She almost fainted while sitting on the side of the bed.

"If you're going to kill me, just do it," she whispered, then closed her eyes against the onslaught.

"Mrs. McTavish, Mary," he said. "May I call you Mary?"

His voice was gentle, calming even. Mary thought it strange coming from a man who was there to murder her. "You're the one with the gun," she said gruffly. "I have no doubt you'll do whatever you want." She pursed her lips and stared at him. She might not be able to stop her death, but she would go down fighting. He studied her. Was that the beginning of a smirk she saw? "What's so funny?" she demanded.

He chuckled, and then he outright laughed. The cheek of the man. "I'm sorry," he told Mary as he continued to laugh. "They didn't warn me you were so…gutsy."

Gutsy? She was not some street thug, she was a refined woman. "How dare you!" she protested, but her voice had begun to waiver. Mary wasn't sure why she was fighting the inevitable. Sooner or later this man who stood in her bridal suite was going to kill her. This was meant to be the happiest day of her life, yet it turned out to be the worst. It would also become her last day on this earth.

He reached into his jacket, and pulled his hand out slowly. Did that mean he was reluctant to kill her? Or at least, to kill her here? There was no way off the train while it was moving, and surely someone would hear the gunshot.

By then, it would be too late. She would be dead, her blood soaking into the luxurious quilt that covered the bed. Mary turned her head to take one more look at it. It had been beautifully made, with not a stitch out of place. It seemed a terrible shame for it to be ruined by her blood. There would be no way to save it.

"Ma'am, Mary," the man said firmly.

Mary glanced up at him again. "Just do it," she said, her voice now breaking up. "I can't stand the pressure."

"Do what?" This time he seemed confused.

Now Mary was confused. "Aren't you here to kill me? I have no idea what Donald did, but it has nothing to do with me."

"I…you've got it all wrong." He shoved something toward her, but the tears forming in her eyes stopped Mary from reading it. She swiped at her eyes—she would not show weakness in front of this man, and must hide her errant tears.

"What is it?" she asked, her voice only slightly above a whisper. Not that it mattered what it was. By the end of the day, she would be dead. Her whirlwind romance with the most handsome man in town was turning out to be the end of her.

"My name is Luke Flanagan. I'm a U.S. Federal Marshal, and I've come to protect you."

Mary had never been so relieved in her life. As she stood, Mary fainted right into the stranger's arms.

Her eyes fluttered open, and Mary stared up into the faces that surrounded her. Luke Flanagan stood over her, along with two strangers. The older man introduced himself as a doctor, who just happened to be traveling on the train. He held a bottle of smelling salts, which had no doubt brought her out of darkness.

"All is well," the doctor said. "I'll leave you to it. Let me know if she deteriorates." He snapped his medical bag closed and left the room.

That cleared up one mystery, but who was the other stranger? Mary began to sit up, and Luke pushed a pillow behind her. "Doc says you need to rest a bit longer," Luke said. That still didn't explain who the other man was. His eyes were firmly fixed on her.

Mary couldn't help but stare back at him. "Mrs. McTavish, Ma'am," he said. "Between the marshal and myself, we'll keep you safe."

She shook her head, trying to clear the cobwebs that had set up home in her mind. "Do I know you?" she asked, still vague on details.

He shoved his large hand toward her. "Peter Jameson, Ma'am. I am the railway detective for this trip." Mary's eyes darted between the two men. Her heart pounded, and she wasn't convinced she wouldn't black out again. It was a lot to take in.

The two men continued to stare down at her. It was unnerving. "Would you both mind giving me some space? I can't breathe. Nor can I think, right at this moment." Mary tried to sit up, but she was still feeling a bit strange.

"Doc said for you to lay down for a bit," Luke said, sounding concerned. Although why he'd be worried about her welfare, Mary had no idea. "When you feel up to it, we need to talk. The three of us," he said, his voice suddenly business-like.

"I'll come back," Peter said. "I'll bring my paperwork with me."

Mary and Luke were suddenly left alone. The room was deathly quiet, and she waited for something awful to happen. And why not? The day was the farthest from the original plan than it could get.

Startled by a knock at the door, Mary sat up abruptly. "Room service," a female voice called.

"That will be tea and cake," Luke said. "The doc wants you to eat." He hurried across to the door, and took the tray from the waitress. "Thank you," he said, then slammed the door closed with his foot.

The suite had a table and two chairs. Luke took the refreshments and placed them on the table. "Do you feel like a cup of tea now?" he asked. "Otherwise, it can wait for a bit."

Tea did sound nice, but Mary didn't want to risk ruining the quilt. Especially after imagining her own blood pouring out onto it. In fact, she wasn't sure she wanted to sleep beneath it tonight. Or ever. She looked down at it with disdain. "I'll come to you," she said firmly, then carefully stood. Mary did not want to faint again.

Meeting her halfway, Luke reached for her hands, then guided her to the table. He pulled out one of the chairs, and helped her to sit. For a moment, Mary felt like an invalid. Except she wasn't sick, and she wasn't feeble either. She was simply in shock. "Thank you, but I am fine, I promise," she told her protector. "Now, tell me what in tarnation is going on?"

Chapter Four

Luke poured tea into the fine China cup, and placed it on the saucer. He pushed it toward Mary and sat opposite her. He then reached for the coffee he'd ordered for himself. "Are you hungry?" he asked, pushing the plate toward her. There was a small selection of sliced cakes and cupcakes. "No matter. Doc wants you to eat something. He seems to think it was brought on by hunger."

"It wasn't hunger. I'm certain it was relief. I thought you'd come to…" She paused for a moment or two, and Luke wasn't sure what she was about to say. "To murder me," Mary said gruffly. "Talk about giving a person a scare." She shook her head, and Luke knew she was right. He went about it the wrong way, given the situation.

In hindsight, he should have accosted her at the McTavish house, and they could have left together. Only he was certain the house would have been watched, which wouldn't have helped their situation. "I acted according to what I believed would work best for the situation." He truly had, but now Luke wondered if he could have done better.

He'd done this job for a very long time now, but nothing prepared him for this particular job. Never had he needed to babysit a new bride, especially someone who clearly had her own ideas on how things should be done.

"It's done now. Nothing we can do about it," she said, waving his words away. Mary daintily sipped her tea, then reached for a cupcake. Luke waited for her to remove her hand before doing the same. There had been little time to eat today. His job had been to follow Donald McTavish and interrogate him. He hadn't even had an opportunity to apprise the sheriff of the situation before McTavish was murdered. The next best thing was to retrieve the dead man's new bride and find out what she knew.

Luke took a mouthful of coffee. The rich beverage slid down his throat, and he savored every moment of it. While they were on the train, they should be safe, but the moment they left, it would be a completely different story. When Rufus Hanson got wind of Mary being in the picture, he would come after her. That was, if he hadn't already.

Knowing the way the criminal thought helped. More likely than not, Rufus would believe Mary knew where his money was. Luke doubted that was true. Asking around town, they barely knew each other. Donald was no doubt using her as cover.

He had to think hard. Where was Donald likely to hide the money? Luke had checked the house in the little time he had, and found nothing. If Mary hadn't run into the bedroom when she did, he would have checked there next. Little did she know, he hid under the bed, and watched her every move.

"Do you know where Donald hid the stolen money?" he demanded.

Mary appeared shocked at the question. "Stolen…money?" She shook her head. "I don't understand."

Luke was convinced she didn't. She was completely innocent of any wrongdoing, and yet here she was, caught up in the middle of all this chaos.

"Mary," he said gently. "Do you know what your husband did for a living?" It was a simple question, requiring an equally simple answer. And yet, once again, she appeared confused.

"I…he…" She thought hard. "I think Donald might have told me he was an accountant?" Her words were matter-of-fact, as though there was nothing wrong with that.

"He was an accountant. This is not going to be easy, but you need to understand the full impact of your husband's actions." He reached across the table and held Mary's hands. "Donald McTavish was an accountant for criminals." He ignored Mary's gasp, and continued with his explanation. "He hid the money from crimes. He mostly worked for Rufus

Hanson. You have surely heard of the Hanson Gang?"

Mary was already pale, but was even more ashen now. If ever he thought she would faint, it would be at this moment. Luke went to stand by her side. "Take a sip of tea," he suggested. When she lifted the cup, tea spilled over the sides. His hands covered hers, stopping the shaking so she could drink.

It was then he heard a knock at the door. Luke stiffened.

"Luke," a male voice called. "It's Peter Jameson." He relaxed, knowing the railway detective was here to help.

He unlocked the door and let the detective in. Peter carried a clipboard that held a handful of papers. "I've got everything. This part was easy," he said, waving the clipboard about. "The tickets proved to be a little more difficult."

Luke sighed. He didn't expect any of it to be easy, and knew it would take quite a bit of time and effort to achieve. Sitting on the side of the bed, Peter pulled out two tickets, then showed them to Luke. "Here are your new tickets," he said, handing them over. "Mr. and Mrs. Luke Flanagan."

Mary's eyes went straight to the proffered tickets, her eyes wide in astonishment. "What are you talking about?" she demanded. "I am not married to Luke. I'm Mrs. McTavish."

"Not anymore," Luke said. "It's our cover. Peter here, has updated the passenger list as well. The McTavish name has been completely removed from all lists connected to this train." He indicated for Peter to sit at the table, while Luke sat on the edge of the bed.

Mary put her head in her hands. "This can't be happening," she mumbled. "This was supposed to be the happiest day of my life."

Luke sighed. He understood it would be a difficult transition, but they had to do this. Pretend they were married, otherwise Mary would be a sitting duck. "Mary," he said gently. "We are trying to protect you. The McTavish name is tarnished, and will be the death of you. Especially if Rufus Hanson gets wind you are on this train."

He almost missed Mary shaking her head it was so minute. "To think I'd fallen in love with that man!" she growled. "And this is how he repays me!"

If the situation hadn't been so serious, it would have been laughable, but this was no laughing matter. Mary McTavish was in danger of losing her life. "Forget McTavish. You are what's important now. From this moment on, we are married. We are on our honeymoon, and will stay in this suite for the most part."

Peter leaned forward. "I've arranged for all your meals to be delivered to your suite," he said. "Anything you require, just ask." He stood to leave, then paused. "It's not unusual with honeymooners," he said. "No one will ask questions as a result." He was quickly gone, leaving the pair alone.

"I know it's difficult," he began, but Mary interrupted him.

She scowled. "You know nothing about how I feel," she snapped. Then her face softened. "I'm sorry— you are only trying to help. This is the most difficult and dangerous situation I've ever found myself in." She studied Luke for a long moment, until he began to squirm. "Will I come out of this alive?"

His shock at her words had him reeling. "If I have anything to say about it, you will." He stepped toward her and pulled Mary from the chair. Then he wrapped her in his arms. The moment she leaned against him, Luke knew he was in trouble.

Keeping his distance was a far better option.

Chapter Five

Mary relaxed into Luke's arms. She knew it was wrong—they weren't married, and she had no right to pretend they were. For this moment, she would go along with the pretense. If it made her feel better, why not?

Moments later, she pulled away. "Are you married, Luke?" she demanded. If he was, then she was effectively the *other* woman. She could not be a party to that. Making him cheat on his wife was wrong on so many levels.

Luke laughed. "No wife," he said. She relaxed back into his arms, knowing full well it was still wrong.

Except it made her feel better, and she could stay there forever. For a minute there, it was as though they belonged together, but Mary knew Luke was merely doing the job he was paid to do. Albeit dangerous.

No wonder he wasn't married. A man like Luke wouldn't want to risk his wife becoming a widow. His job was far too dangerous. "Would you ever get married?" she asked, her voice almost a whisper.

He laughed, forcing her to move out of his arms. "Are you offering?" he asked, his mirth clear in his voice.

"What? And become a widow and new bride in quick succession?" She shook her head. At least she knew he was joking.

Suddenly, the laughter stopped. "You know, that's not a bad idea. We will be stuck on this train, in this room, for the duration of the trip."

Mary's heart thudded. "For the entire two weeks?"

"For the entire two weeks. I can't risk you being recognized. You might be safe in the lounge of the Pullman car, but it's a risk I'd rather not take." He pulled her close again, and although Mary felt comforted, she wasn't sure they should be doing this.

"Where…" She swallowed. "Where will you sleep?" she asked, glancing around the room. There were two comfortable chairs along with the chairs at the table. Apart from that, there was the bed. If they were married, they would share the bed. But they weren't, and it would be a sin for her to sleep with Luke. Even if it was deemed necessary. Mary swallowed again—her throat felt dry, and panic was beginning to set in.

Her heart pounding, Mary pulled away from Luke. She headed toward one of the comfortable chairs, where she wanted to be swallowed whole. Perhaps she could get off at the next stop and take her chances? Or maybe she would demand Luke leave her to her own devices. He couldn't force her to accept his protection. Could he?

"It's not so bad," Luke said. "We get along pretty good. You don't exactly hate me, do you?" When she glanced up into his face, Luke was grinning. Mary wanted nothing more than to slap that grin right off his face.

Of course, she was too much of a lady to do so. "I don't hate you," she said, choosing her words carefully. "The problem is, we're not married." Now that she'd laid her cards on the table, Luke couldn't deny it. "I can't share a room, or a bed, with a man I'm not married to."

He raised his eyebrows. Luke seemed thoughtful. "I can easily fix that," he said. "I'll arrange for us to be married."

The shock of his words hit her like a bullet had slammed into her. Mary was speechless. Since her words made him come to that conclusion, there was little she could do about it.

Her only hope was there was no preacher on the train.

~*~

Less than an hour later, Luke Flanagan and Mary McTavish were pronounced man and wife.

Mary still reeled from the shock. One day, two weddings. She prayed this one didn't end the same way as the first one. From what she'd been told, Donald deserved what he'd been dished out. Luke did not.

Despite the ceremony that was quickly thrown together, she wasn't certain she wanted to sleep with Luke. They were complete strangers—she'd met him only hours ago. At least with Donald, she'd known him longer.

Little good that had done for her. He had secrets that led not only to his death, but put her in extreme danger.

Peter and the conductor acted as witnesses. They were the only people who knew the situation. And now the preacher did too. Both Peter and Luke demanded the man must not divulge their marriage, as it would put Mary in grave danger. He agreed.

"I've arranged for a special meal for you," Peter told them. "I'll bring it to you myself. Chef is making something special for the honeymooners."

She must have looked shocked, because he quickly added, "All the staff knew we had honeymooners traveling with us. This suite is mostly booked by newlyweds."

Mary felt her breath leave her body her relief was so intense. "Thank you," she said, then stepped toward Luke. He had become her savior, her protector, and she'd come to rely on him.

When she thought about it, relying on him that way was not necessarily a good thing. If something happened to him, heaven forbid, she would be alone again. His arm wrapped around her back, and she couldn't move away. If she was truthful with herself, Mary was comforted by his presence. When he held her, there was a whole new level to the way she felt.

Knowing it was wrong, although they were now married, she didn't try to pull away. Once she was safe, they would deal with the fallout. Annulments were easy to get, Luke told her. Especially when it was a situation like this.

It made her wonder if he'd married his charge before. He only smiled when she asked the question, making her wonder even more.

Her pretend husband was a sly one. She'd have to watch out for him. Especially when it came time for bed.

Chapter Six

Peter and the others had only been gone a short time when there was a knock at the door. "Room service," a female voice called. Luke ushered Mary out of sight. Hand on his gun, he slowly opened the door.

The waitress smiled at him. "Compliments of the chef," she said. "He loves to make something special for our honeymooners." This time her smile was wide, and she pushed the food trolley toward him. "Would you like me to serve it? I'm happy to do so."

Luke grinned. "Thank you, but we can do it ourselves." He wiggled his eyebrows trying to send a message the waitress would understand, even if it wasn't true.

She chuckled. "Whatever you prefer, Sir." She then left him to wheel the trolley in himself.

Closing and locking the door behind him, Luke wheeled the trolley to the table. "Hungry?" he asked. Of course she was hungry. Mary had barely eaten anything today. At least in the time he'd been with her.

"Not really," Mary answered, but strolled to the table anyway.

Lifting the lids from the food, Luke breathed in the delicious aroma. "Roasted beef with gravy and vegetables. Smells amazing." He replaced that lid, then moved over to the desserts. "The chef really has gone out of his way for us," he said. "I feel bad about that. Then again, we really are newlyweds." He grinned then. Mary scowled. "You don't like Charlotte Russe?" he asked, as he covered the glorious dessert once more. Luke shrugged.

"I…I do," Mary said. "What I don't like is being deceitful."

Stepping toward her, and helping Mary into her chair, didn't seem to appease his new wife. "We are married. We may not be in love, but we are legally joined in holy matrimony. By a preacher, no less."

"I happened to be there at the time," she snapped. "I am not a dishonest person, and I hate lies."

She glared at him then, making Luke feel more than a little uneasy. "Sometimes we have to do things that make us uncomfortable. Your life is at stake— keep that in mind. It really is a life or death situation, make no mistake."

Mary went deathly white. While he felt guilty about scaring her, it needed to be done. Why was it Mary didn't believe she was in danger? Heck, they could have murdered her when they killed Donald McTavish. It was pure luck they hadn't.

She visibly shuddered, adding yet another layer of guilt. "You're right," she said firmly. "I apologize for my behavior." Despite her words, Mary continued to glare, making Luke wonder how sorry she really was.

If he'd learned anything about his new wife, he already knew she would say whatever she thought. She wouldn't accept lies or cover-ups, and she was feisty as heck. He almost chuckled at the last thought, but it was neither the time or the place.

Instead, he placed her food in front of Mary.

She leaned in. "It does smell wonderful," she said, then reached for his hand.

Luke was a Christian, but with his job rarely got to church. He appreciated the chance to be put back on track. No doubt, in the time they had together, Mary McTavish, er, Flanagan, would steer him in the right direction.

Like it or not.

~*~

Luke leaned back and patted his belly. "That's the best meal I've had for a very long time," he said. Mary ate most of her meal, and he was happy with that. "Chef certainly went all out for us."

Wiping her lips with the linen napkin, Mary seemed somewhat withdrawn. "As much as the food was wonderful, I still feel bad."

"Please don't," Luke told her. "We are married, and that's what everyone on board believes." Mary sighed and Luke could feel her frustration. "I know you hate lies, but it's not a lie. Our marriage might be fake, but we are still married. That means we are not lying."

He studied her, but Mary showed no sign of agreeing with him. Then she shrugged her shoulders. "I guess so," she said, but Luke could tell she didn't really believe him. What would it take for her to feel better about the deception? They were in an extremely difficult situation, but he wasn't convinced his wife understood that.

Luke shuddered. *His wife.* It wasn't something he ever thought he would say. For all of his adult life, Luke had been a marshal. It wasn't the safest job, and most of his colleagues avoided marriage like the plague. There were long assignments that meant they were gone from home, sometimes for weeks or months at a time. That was not conducive to a good marriage. Then, if there were children involved, they didn't get to know their father.

And that didn't even touch on the danger that came with the job. Being shot, or heaven forbid, killed, was not a good ending to a marriage that was already challenging. The entire scenario was difficult for all concerned.

It was the reason Luke would arrange for an annulment the moment the danger was over. That way, Mary would have the freedom to marry again if that's what she decided to do.

He glanced across at her. "You look tired. Exhausted even. Why don't you go to bed?" The moment the words were out, she appeared uncomfortable. After a few seconds' delay, Luke realized why—their sleeping arrangements hadn't been discussed. It would be playing on her mind. "I'll settle in the chair," he said, pointing to the comfortable lounge chair not far from the bed.

She nodded, then headed into the bathroom. Being the best of the private suites available, they had the luxury of their own bathroom. Donald McTavish must have paid a fortune for it, Luke decided. Exactly how much he would probably never know, but he was certain it would outweigh Luke's monthly wage, if not more.

He felt bad for Mary. She went into her marriage with McTavish not knowing what she was getting herself into. Luke felt compelled to snatch her up before her marriage ceremony with her groom, but that was not allowed. Showing himself and declaring he was a federal marshal was not allowed.

Keeping a low profile until they could interview her new husband were his orders. No doubt McTavish would have ended up in jail after that, leaving Mary in a precarious position. However, it would not have been as dangerous as it was now.

He packed up the soiled dishes onto the tray and cautiously opened the door. No one was around, and he wheeled the trolley outside their room, where one of the waitresses would collect it later. Luke could hear Mary puttering about in the bathroom, and wondered what she was doing. No doubt having a good wash. It had certainly been a difficult day for her. Unfortunately, things could easily get worse.

When she opened the bathroom door, he glanced across at his new wife. She was beautiful, even in her nightgown and robe. "Turn around," she told him, and Luke complied. "You can turn back now," Mary told him moments later.

When he did so, she was in bed and her silk robe was on the end of the bed. Luke had no doubt McTavish had lashed out and purchased a whole new wardrobe of clothes for his soon-to-be wife. What he knew of the man, McTavish wouldn't allow himself to be seen with a wife who wore cheap clothes. Before their marriage, Mary had worked at the mercantile. She could no more afford to buy a silk robe than Luke could. He wondered if she'd realized everything he'd bought her was with blood money.

Luke shook his head. Mary was far too naïve for her own good. There was no way she would have worked that out. He didn't want to be the one to tell her.

42

Chapter Seven

It felt like forever before she finally settled, but Mary knew she had to relax if she wanted to fall asleep.

Having Luke watching her every move was not helping. The other thing that held her back was knowing tonight was her wedding night, yet the man she'd married this morning was dead. And now she was married to a complete stranger. One who identified himself as a federal agent.

Worse still, she now realized, Mary had not asked him for any identification. What if he was the man who had killed Donald?

A shudder went through her, and Mary suddenly sat up. "Show me your badge," she demanded.

Luke's lips quivered as he tried to hold back a smile. Reaching into his jacket pocket, he pulled an item out, then stepped toward her. "I did try to show it to you earlier, but you fainted. I wondered how long it would take you to ask," he said.

Fury burned inside her. Why hadn't he offered it to her since then? More importantly, why hadn't she thought of it? Except she knew there was a very good reason—she was in shock. Her husband, her first husband of the day, Douglas McTavish, was murdered in front of her. Right on the steps of the courthouse.

She barely had time to think before running to the home they were to share. Mary reached out and took the badge Luke handed to her. She stared at it for what seemed a lifetime. Her mind was in a fog. What should she be looking for? It could be a fake badge for all she knew.

If that were the case, wouldn't the railway detective have spotted it? Surely that would have been the case.

"It's not fake," he finally said. "Peter Jameson has checked it out. You would have been informed if I wasn't who I said I was." He reached out a hand to take it back. "In fact, I'd be sitting in the tiny jail cell they have hidden on the train."

Mary felt relief. Of course, the railway detective would have known if the badge was not real. "I…I'm sorry. I guess my nerves have got the better of me." Their hands brushed as Luke took back his badge. Something went through her at that moment, but Mary had no idea what it was. It was then she realized she sat in the bed, with the top half of herself showing. Normally, the bedding would be held up in front of her. Any normal, decent woman would do that, right?

Of course she would. Mary snatched up the blankets and covered herself.

Luke chuckled.

Mary glared at him. So much for her wedding night. One groom dead, and the other sitting in a chair on the opposite side of the room. Her eyes filled with tears. The impact of the day finally hit her. "Donald really is dead?" she asked quietly. Her voice faltered, and Luke's head shot up.

He sat on the side of the bed next to her. "I'm afraid so," he told her, then reached out and brushed her tears away. "It's a lot to take in, I know. Tomorrow will be better, you'll see." Only Mary didn't believe him. She would still be in hiding, and still fighting to stay alive.

"The man who killed Donald, why is he after me? I've done nothing, and I know even less." Her heart felt heavy at the thought someone had decided she needed to die. Simply because she'd married Donald McTavish.

"My first thought was money, but now I believe he's looking for evidence of some kind. The sort of evidence that would implicate the killer if it were found by the authorities. Pure stupidity on your late husband's behalf."

He shrugged then, and Mary wasn't certain what to think. If they were looking for evidence, why threaten her? "Are you certain they're after me?"

Luke studied her for a long moment. "We're not certain, but we have to cover all possibilities. My guess is Donald threatened Rufus Hanson with something. And now Hanson believes you're a threat. He will do what he does best—eliminate the threat."

Mary gasped and slapped her hands to her mouth. She felt the color drain from her face, and suddenly felt faint. Surely Luke didn't mean that?

"I'm sorry," he said quickly. "I shouldn't have said that. The last thing I wanted to do was scare you."

Mary lay back down in the bed. "It's far too late for that," she whispered, then turned away from him. If she thought sleep was elusive before, it would be even more difficult now.

Luke reached out and took her hand. "Mary," he said quietly. "I truly am sorry. You seem like the sort of person who wants the truth. I am someone who doesn't like to lie to the people I'm protecting. Surely that counts for something?"

For some strange reason, Mary felt sorry for Luke in that moment. He appeared truly contrite. How could she blame him for doing what she demanded? The reality was, she couldn't. She closed her eyes momentarily. "You're right," she whispered. "I prefer the truth. I hate liars." Mary sat up again then. Sleep was obviously going to elude her tonight. Why she even bothered, Mary had no idea.

Apart from the trauma of the day, a man she didn't know, and yet, had married without much thought, shared the suite she was meant to share with her husband. Her first husband, Donald.

Mary's wedding day had suddenly become chaotic and filled with danger. It was a far cry from the peaceful wedding Donald had planned for the pair.

~*~

Sleep had eluded her until the early hours of the morning. The knock at the door was the only reason Mary was awake now. "Breakfast," she heard muffled through the door, then movement next to her on the bed.

She turned to glance at her new husband, Donald. Only it wasn't Donald she saw, but Luke. He was fully dressed and lay on top of the bedding, so she guessed that was something. He sat up, then turned to face her. "Good morning," he said, then went to the door.

Mary noticed the gun under his jacket as he stood, sending shivers down her spine. This was her new reality. For a moment, she'd thought it all a dream. Instead, it was a nightmare, and she was living it.

"Thank you," Luke said, then shut and locked the door behind him. As he'd done last night, the trolley was placed next to the table. He lifted the lid on one of the plates. "It smells delicious," he told her. Mary could smell it from the bed, and couldn't wait to eat it.

"Bacon, sausages and eggs, with toast," he said. "There is also oatmeal and juice, coffee and tea. Oh, and hot biscuits." She watched as he placed a small platter of fruit in the middle of the table.

"There's enough food there to feed an entire family," she said. "We won't get through all of that."

Luke didn't say a word, just smiled, then turned his back as she climbed out of bed. Reaching for her robe, she hurried into the bathroom to ready herself for breakfast. Mary had never been so idle in her life. If the circumstances had been different, she probably would have enjoyed it. As it stood, she couldn't relax, and certainly wouldn't enjoy even a moment of the enforced confinement she found herself in.

Mary couldn't wait for the day Rufus Hanson was arrested, and she could mourn Donald. Her status was rather confusing. She'd gone from widow to new bride in less than a day. Where did that leave her?

"Ready to eat?" Luke asked as she exited the bathroom. He was in the midst of pouring tea from the fancy pot.

Her eyes gazed at the trolley, and Mary was taken aback. From Luke's description, she already knew there was a lot of food, but hadn't realized quite how much. All she really wanted was a decent cup of tea. Most of these places didn't serve good tea.

Luke helped Mary into her chair, then went around to the other side of the table, where he poured coffee for himself. "It really is decadent, isn't it?" he asked, a wide grin on his face. "I can't say I'm unhappy with this assignment."

It was then it hit Mary. Of course, she was nothing more to him than an assignment. And when it was over, when Donald's killer was caught, they would get an annulment and go their separate ways. How long that would take was the question. She only hoped it was sooner rather than later. Being in such close proximity for the next two weeks couldn't be good for either of them.

Mary sighed and sipped her tea. As it slowly slid down her throat, she silently praised whoever had prepared her pot of tea. They were absolute angels.

Chapter Eight

Luke watched Mary over the top of his mug. She seemed to savor the tea, as he knew she would. He had no idea why, but the humble cup of tea seemed to soothe the nerves. Coffee did the same for him.

He hadn't slept much last night—at least while he was in that chair. As much as it was likely the most luxurious chair he'd ever had the pleasure to sit in, it wasn't made for many hours of sleep. It especially wasn't constructed for someone of his substantial height. In the early hours of the morning, once Mary was sound asleep, he slipped off his shoes and lay down next to her. It wasn't long before he, too, was asleep.

The thing that surprised him was Mary not mentioning his presence next to her last night. Luke was certain it would be a sticking point. He decided, it had instead comforted her to know he was close to hand, should something untoward occur.

Uncovering the plates of hot food, he offered the first to Mary. "I'm not hungry," she told him quietly.

"Perhaps not, but you need to keep up your strength. Even a little is better than nothing," he almost pleaded. The last thing he needed was a fainting woman on his hands due to a lack of food. Immediately, as the thought entered his mind, Luke silently admonished himself. This was a challenging situation, and he needed to have more compassion.

Some days, this job was just that, a job. Other times, he felt more connected to the people he protected. Mary was difficult to get to know. It was completely understandable. She'd been through absolute hell and all within the same day. As she stood next to the man she'd expected to live out the rest of her life with, he'd been murdered in front of her eyes.

Luke couldn't even begin to imagine the fear she had experienced. Pure evil stood somewhere close by, and could have easily killed Mary for being in the wrong place at the wrong time. It was pure luck she wasn't dead now.

The thought made him shudder. An innocent bystander, as Mary was, should not have to endure such terror. Donald McTavish did the entirely wrong thing bringing Mary into his dangerous world. From what Luke had been told, he was greedy. Working for criminals, compiling evidence, and especially stealing from them, was the worst thing he could have done.

Surely the man knew he would put his bride in jeopardy? Did he have no conscience?

Apparently not. His type was both evil and selfish—they took what they wanted, no matter the cost. In this case, the cost was not only his life, but the threat of his widow's life.

Luke knew he would do everything in his power to keep Mary safe. As though she was his own wife.

It was then it hit him—she really was his wife, and he wasn't exactly unhappy about it. Pushing a bowl of oatmeal toward Mary, he watched as she screwed up her face. It was unbecoming, or so he'd been told, but it pleased Luke she felt comfortable enough with him to do so. He couldn't help but chuckle. "Try a little?" he asked quietly. "You need to keep up your strength." She stared at him quizzically then, and Mary studied him. *In case we need to flee*, he wanted to say, but restrained himself. Luke truly hoped it didn't come to that.

Picking up the spoon, Mary plunged it into the bowl. She put a small amount into her mouth. Again, she pulled a face. Luke reached across the table and handed her the honey. "Perhaps a little honey might help?" he suggested. "Do you like milk on your oatmeal?" He indicated the ornate jug filled with fresh milk. "It doesn't matter what you eat, but you need to eat. I hate picking up fainting women off the floor," he joked. In reality, it was a real concern.

"I don't like oatmeal much," she told him. Despite her words, Mary lifted the honey and poured a little over the near flavorless food. She stirred it in, then took another mouthful. "Better, but not what I'd call appetizing." Mary sighed, then gazed across the table at the remaining offerings.

Luke reached for her hand. "There is plenty here to choose from, but if you have a particular preference, I'm certain the chef will make something for you."

Shaking her head, Mary reached for the plate of fruit. "I don't want him to go to any trouble for me. This will be fine," she said, taking a bite of an apple.

As he watched her closely, Luke knew he was fussing. But wasn't that his job? To ensure her well-being in addition to her safety? If he didn't do the first, then the second was impossible. "I have an idea," he said, the thought popping into his mind. "I'll request menus, and we can choose our meals. Donald paid handsomely for this trip, and I'm sure there are options."

Mary shook her head in protest. "It's not necessary," she said firmly.

"Oh, but it is," Luke replied. "I will not allow you to fade away like a wilted flower right in front of my eyes." He grinned, trying to make light of the situation, but despite their short time together, he already knew Mary was not one to make a fuss. That meant it was up to him to ensure she was well looked after.

Pleased that she was finally eating, Luke tucked into his own breakfast. He wondered what today would bring. He hoped and prayed it would be a peaceful day for all concerned.

Especially Mary. His new bride.

Chapter Nine

Mary was bored. There was nothing to do stuck here in their suite. Well, the suite that was meant to be hers and Donald's. At least with Donald, there would have been things to do. They could have gone to the lounge area, and mingled with other passengers. Meals could be taken in the main dining area.

Watching out the windows at the passing scenery would have filled at least some of her idle time. Luke had already excluded all those activities, much to Mary's annoyance. There was a small window in their suite, but she was banned from pulling back the curtain. That meant she had no option but to sit and do nothing. "There must be something we can do," she said gruffly. "This is meant to be my honeymoon. Instead, I am bored to tears. I don't even have a book to read." She pouted then, much to her dismay. Mary was not one to pout or even grumble, but she was pushed beyond her limits.

Luke frowned. "I'm not sure what there is to do. I could request a book for you, but I couldn't guarantee it was to your taste."

Forcing herself not to sigh, Mary did her best to be gracious. "That would be lovely. Thank you, Luke," she said, then went back to staring at her hands.

A knock at the door startled her. "It's Peter Jameson," a voice called through the door. Mary felt immediate relief. Not that she had a reason to be scared. Luke was right there with her, his gun hidden under the jacket he wore constantly. It was then she did a double take. When had he removed his jacket?

What she saw now was his tall frame opening the door. His muscles bulging against his crisp white shirt, and a holster in full view. She really must be bored, not even noticing the change. Especially when it piqued her interest, which was the last thing Mary wanted.

"Come in," Luke told their visitor, then stepped aside for the railway detective to enter.

"Mrs. Flanagan," Peter said as he entered the room. "I have menus for you. I'm sorry the meals so far haven't been to your liking. You should have been provided with menus from the moment you arrived, so I must apologize."

For Mary, the unsaid words were someone didn't do their job properly. The moment the thought entered her mind, Mary knew she was being uncharitable. With everything else that happened from the moment Luke joined her in the suite, she wasn't at all surprised menus were overlooked. There had been a whirlwind of activity, to the point her head spun. "Thank you," she said meekly, reaching for the menus. "I hope you didn't go to too much trouble."

He smiled, and Mary felt herself relax. "Not at all. I'm only sorry it was overlooked. Is there anything else I can get to help relieve the boredom?"

Luke indicated for Peter to sit down. "We've just been discussing that very thing," he said. "Is there a library of sorts on the train? Mary is pushed to her limits with the monotony."

Peter scratched his head momentarily, then smiled again. "I do believe there is a small library. What sort of books do you like? I'll see what I can do."

"Romance is always welcome," she said brightly. "I used to like reading those penny crime novels too. Now I feel like I'm living in one, so I'll give that a miss." She shook her head then. "Honestly, at this point, I'll take anything you can get your hands on. Anything at all."

Beggars can't be choosers, or so her mother always said, but Mary always thought otherwise. Recent events had proven that old saying to be correct. At least for now. She only hoped the situation was short-lived and life would soon return to normal.

"Romance it is," Peter said as he stood. "I'll be back as soon as I find something suitable. If you have the time…" He paused then and grinned. "Let me start over—please look over the menus and I'll take your orders back to the chef in time for lunch."

Mary smiled then. It was the first time in days she found something to smile about, and it made her heart happy. "I'll definitely do that," she said firmly. "I appreciate you taking the time."

Peter nodded briefly, then shook Luke's hand. The two men headed for the door. She'd had a brief reprieve from the boredom, and now she at least had something to do. Her eyes scrolled down the variety of food. Several items caught her attention, and Mary reached into a drawer for pen and paper.

If she could fill her belly, Mary knew she would be far more content. She had accepted the situation, and could do nothing to change it. Things were beginning to look up.

Mary looked up from the book she'd been reading. The knock at the door was a welcomed reprieve. The book Peter Jameson had chosen for her piqued her interest, but reading only kept her attention for so long.

"Room service," a female voice called through the door.

Luke shrugged on his jacket. It would never do for the help to see his firearm. It would give away far too much. Mary watched as he opened the door, her heart pounding. Despite the fact Peter had assured them all the staff were regulars, and all passengers checked, she was still wary. It wasn't surprising.

"I'll take it in, thank you," she heard Luke say. He then deftly rolled the food trolley into their suite. He lifted the lid to the main course and placed Mary's meal in front of her. "Looks good, and smells even better," he told her.

Luke placed the beef stew in front of her, and Mary leaned in, inhaling the enticing aroma. She glanced up at Luke and smiled. "Thank you for organizing this," she said, then waited patiently for him to sit opposite her.

"It was all Peter," he said. "I should have thought of it earlier. I'm really sorry."

He seemed contrite, although none of this was his fault. "Please don't apologize," Mary said, then reached out for his hand. At first Luke seemed reluctant to take her hand, but only momentarily until he realized what she was doing. "Lord, we thank you for this food, when many would be doing without. Thank you also for sending Luke to protect me. Amen."

She let go of his hand, and instantly regretted it. Until that moment, Mary hadn't realized how safe she felt in his presence. As he held her, that feeling was even more heightened. It was peculiar to her, since Luke Flanagan was but a stranger. And yet, she placed her entire life and her very being in his hands.

Mary had to trust him—he was a marshal after all.

Lifting her fork, Mary took a mouthful of the aromatic stew. She savored the delicious food, the beef melting in her mouth. As she reached for more, she noticed Luke grinning. "I guess you like it," he said, laughter in his voice.

"It is the best beef stew I've ever eaten," she said, then went back to her meal.

If the food continued to be this good, Mary was certain she could endure her enforced confinement with her pretend husband.

Chapter Ten

Luke could take this treatment any day.

He had to admit their earlier meals were not necessarily to his taste, but they were still enjoyable. With the array of enticing foods now available to them, they were in heaven. Luke knew for a fact he was, and going by Mary's reaction, she was too.

And that was what mattered most—that she was happy and comfortable. Not to mention safe and protected. It went without saying he would protect her with his very life. It was his job.

Except something was different this time. He had protected many people in the years he'd been a marshal, many of them women. Not once had he married any of those women to ensure their protection. However, this was a totally different situation.

Wasn't it?

Thinking about it, he wasn't so sure. The railway detective had changed the paperwork to ensure Mary's true identity was kept hidden. Which begged the question, why did he marry his charge?

She'd insisted they marry if they were to share the room, but that wasn't the real reason. There was definitely something about Mary. It wasn't only that she was scared. Terrified in fact. He felt drawn to her the moment he'd laid eyes on her at the courthouse. It wasn't as though he knew she was marrying the crime accountant, because he didn't. They'd each gone there under their own steam. It wasn't until he was inside the courthouse, did Luke discover they went there to marry. By then, it was too late to stop it.

Not that he had the power to do that, but he'd felt sorry for the young woman McTavish had married quietly and without fanfare. Not because there was no big celebration, but because she was the innocent party in the dangerous scenario.

Dangerous because intelligence had told them McTavish was a target. It was the very reason Luke had been sent to speak with the man. Adding a wife to the mix made it all the more dangerous. For her.

In Luke's opinion, Donald McTavish deserved all he got, but not Mary. He had suspected she didn't know about McTavish's business or his lifestyle, and he'd been proven right.

"The bread is still warm," Mary said, her delight apparent. She reached for the butter and added it to the bread. It looked truly delicious.

Luke reached out and added a slice of bread to his plate. Mary passed him the butter. When their hands connected, he felt a zing run up his arm. Mary's eyes opened wide. But only momentarily. She studied him briefly, then went back to eating.

"How was your stew?" she asked without looking at him.

He glanced up. "It was truly delicious," he told her. "I'm sure dessert will be equally tasty." Luke placed his soiled dishes on the tray, and placed the desserts on the table. "Cherry cobbler for two," he said, adding a bowl of clotted cream between them.

Mary finished up, and added her soiled dishes to the trolley, then poured her tea. "Do you think Rufus Hanson will ever give up trying to kill me?" she asked, her voice wavering.

Luke's heart thudded. The last thing he wanted was for her to distress herself with worry about Hanson. "He'll be behind bars the moment we catch up with him. In the meantime, I'm here to ensure your safety." Luke reached out and covered her hand, hoping it would be enough to reassure her. "Eat up," he said quietly. "It looks enticing." It wasn't a lie— the food was beyond anything he'd had before.

He enjoyed what they'd had previously, but for Mary, it just wasn't to her tastes. Now, though, he thoroughly appreciated knowing she was content with the meals. He glanced at her over the top of his coffee mug. She sipped her tea daintily. For someone who worked at the mercantile, Mary was proving herself to be a real lady.

That lady was his wife. Luke was certain he could get used to it. Only he knew he shouldn't and definitely mustn't. There was an annulment on their horizon. If they became too close, it would break both their hearts.

Once the meal was over, Mary stacked all the remaining soiled plates on the trolley. Luke rolled it outside their door, where he knew the waitress would come along later and collect it. He glanced about at the other passengers wandering about after finishing their midday meal. They went about their business as though nothing was amiss.

And yet, Luke had a feeling of foreboding. His biggest fear was Rufus Hanson had somehow found his way onto the train and was waiting to pounce. Except he'd been reassured that was not the case. The railway detective had checked every passenger and verified their identity. It wasn't something he did often, but it was done from time to time. Especially when there was a high-profile passenger on the train.

That being the case, why wouldn't he let Mary go out and mingle with the other passengers? Luke shook himself mentally. It wasn't an option. Even with him by her side, should something go awry, it would put the other passengers in danger.

He would not risk it. Plus, knowing Mary, she wouldn't want to do that either. She was a kind and gentle soul. If nothing else, he'd learned that about her.

Besides, who was to say Hanson hadn't sent someone else to spy? He had the money and the resources to do so. The thought immediately put Luke on high alert. Why hadn't he thought of it before?

The only person Luke was certain he could trust was the railway detective. If he was cynical, he would worry about his legitimacy, too. But Peter Jameson seemed very genuine and had bent over backwards to help them out.

Luke shook his head to clear away the thought. Except the revelation lingered, and he had no way of knowing the truth.

"I'm going to lay down for a while," Mary announced, pulling Luke out of his dark thoughts. Why he'd begun to think this way, he didn't know. What he did know was this case had become personal. Mary was not only someone he was sent to protect, she was now his wife. Their marriage might only be fake, and for the sake of making her happy, but it was real in the eyes of the law.

Turning to face her, Luke worried about her health. "Are you alright? Should I call for the doctor?"

Mary rolled her eyes. "I am perfectly fine. I'm simply tired from doing nothing."

Luke understood completely. Boredom did that to a person. His job caused a lot of boredom. Sitting around doing nothing wasn't the most entertaining job, but it had to be done. Besides, after a while, you get used to it. He was always on high alert while he was working, so it was nothing new. He was grateful being here on the train, in the Pullman car and in the large suite McTavish had booked and paid for. It meant they were contained and away from the rest of the passengers.

And that was exactly what was needed in this situation. Unfortunately, it wouldn't last beyond the two weeks originally booked.

Chapter Eleven

There was only so much reading a woman could do. As much as she adored reading, Mary knew she couldn't read for all of her waking moments.

She removed her shoes and lay down on the bed. It didn't take long for her eyes to droop and for Mary to fall into a deep sleep.

Awaking with a start, she found the railway detective in the room. Where was Luke? She couldn't see him anywhere. Panic set in, and she sat up abruptly.

"You're awake," Peter said quietly. "Luke will be back shortly."

Mary studied him. She wasn't convinced Luke would leave her alone for any reason. Except perhaps if she was in danger and he went after the culprit. "Where is he?" She had a right to know, after all.

Peter licked his lips before answering. "Luke had to check something. He won't be long."

The railway detective's words did not appease Mary. Her heart rate increased and she was suddenly panicking. "He…Luke wouldn't leave me alone," she sputtered, her words wary, even to her own ears.

Peter stood, his tall height overwhelming her. "I promise you," he said, taking a step toward her, "Luke won't be long. He simply needed to do some checking."

Why Mary was fearful at that moment, she didn't know, but it felt like she'd been put in the hands of a killer. How did she know Peter Jameson wasn't really Rufus Hanson? Or one of his henchmen? The thought hadn't crossed her mind until now.

"Can I get you something? A cup of tea, water, lemonade?" He glanced at the trolley sitting close to the table. "It's all there. Here, let me help," he said as she sat on the side of the bed.

It was at that moment Mary knew Peter was trustworthy. If he was a killer, he could have murdered her while she slept. Except he didn't. He had watched over her, and protected her while she replenished her energy, which had been wavering.

"Has the train stopped?" she asked. "We don't seem to be moving."

"It has indeed," Peter told her. "Rather than wake you unnecessarily, Luke asked me to watch over you." He guided Mary to one of the comfortable chairs. "What would you like to drink?" he asked, already stepping toward the refreshments trolley.

"Lemonade sounds refreshing," she said, and watched as he came closer.

He handed her the glass, then offered up a plate of assorted delicacies. "Take your pick," he said. "Have everything if you want. There's plenty here."

At first Mary was taken aback at the suggestion. Then she laughed. Out loud, no less. She was in the most precarious situations she would likely face in her entire life, yet here she was being offered a ridiculous amount of petite delicacies.

Is this what her life amounted to? Being protected on a train headed for she didn't know where, and absurd food to keep her occupied.

Peter stared at her, then joined in the laughter. Mary felt almost hysterical, but didn't care right now. Tears rolled down her face, and she was powerless to stop them.

Without warning, the door opened wide. Peter pulled his gun from his holster. The gun Mary didn't know he was carrying. Luke entered and glanced from one to the other. "Everything alright?" he asked, appearing confused.

Mary's laughter immediately stopped, and she wiped at her face. "Everything is fine," she said, then took a sip of her lemonade as though nothing was amiss.

~*~

"Hanson is off the grid," Luke told Peter quietly.

If he thought Mary couldn't hear him, he was wrong. "Does that mean you don't know where he is?"

Luke glanced at Peter, who shrugged his shoulders.

Mary rolled her eyes.

Why Luke thought she couldn't hear him, she would never know. They might have a suite, but it wasn't so big secrets could be kept from her. "If you have something to say, I want to hear it," Mary demanded. "Whatever affects me, you must tell me."

Again he glanced at Peter. "Not my call," Peter said, his hands up in front of himself, and backing away. "I'm just the babysitter."

His last words annoyed Mary. "I am not a child!" she said firmly. If she'd been standing, Mary knew she would have stomped her foot. Sitting, as she was, didn't lend itself to such an action.

Luke glanced at her then laughed. "You most certainly are not," he said firmly, his eyes burning her with the way he looked her up and down.

"Time for me to go," Peter said, then retreated from the suite, leaving the pair alone.

"Where did you go?" Mary demanded the moment the door closed behind the railway detective. "I was scared when I saw you weren't here." Knowing she was safe, and believing it, were two different things she'd discovered.

"I had to ensure Hanson was not around. It's a long way from Karisvale, but for the gang leader, distance is no obstacle."

Luke's words made her heart pound in her head. "He's still looking for me, isn't he?" she asked, her voice barely above a whisper.

Glancing at her, then down at his hands, he spoke the words Mary didn't want to hear. "As I understand it, he's still looking for you."

This time, her tears were not from laughter, but from fear.

Chapter Twelve

The expression on Mary's face was a kick in the gut. Why he didn't lie to her, Luke did not know. Except deep down he did—he'd become far too fond of his temporary wife. She'd demanded the truth, and he owed it to her. The trouble was, the truth was terrifying.

Luke wasn't sure what he could do except continue what he'd been doing. And that was to protect her day and night. Mary deserved that, and more. She should be happy, enjoying her honeymoon, except the man she'd married was not right for her.

Mary was an angel. She could do no harm to anyone. Why Donald McTavish picked her, Luke would never know. Or did he?

From what he'd learned, McTavish was the type to choose a woman who was naïve about the ways of the world. That was Mary. He'd want someone who would ask no questions. That might be Mary when things went smoothly, but as he'd learned, it was not Mary when she didn't agree.

He almost chuckled at the thought of her standing up to McTavish. He soon sobered at the criminal's reaction. There was no way McTavish would put up with a woman who challenged him. Luke understood the man could be violent when it was called for, but would he attack his wife?

The truth was, Luke decided, he likely would.

As much as the man's death was a shock to his new bride, she was far better off without him. Except Rufus Hanson erroneously assumed Mary knew all about McTavish's business, which she didn't.

He glanced across at Mary. What he saw broke his heart. Tears flooded her cheeks, and her face was red from crying. It wasn't something he had planned to evoke, but Luke knew it was his fault. He could have said Hanson was no longer looking for her. Except it would be a lie, one that would put her in danger. Knowing Mary the way he did, she would demand she leave the train. It wasn't an option.

Reaching into his pocket, Luke handed her his clean handkerchief. "Don't cry," he said gently. "I won't let him near you. We've wiped out any record of McTavish being on this train, so he has no way to locate you." Even so, Luke knew it may not be enough. Hanson had spies everywhere. At least he knew Peter Jameson was trustworthy. Background checks had been carried out on the railway detective, and Luke now knew he was previously a marshal. It was a huge relief.

Squatting down next to Mary, he felt her pain. They may not have known each other long, only a matter of days, but he had become quite fond of the woman who was now his wife.

But only temporarily, he reminded himself. Why that upset Luke, he wasn't sure.

Mary was such a sweet person. That had to be the reason. He watched as she wiped her tears away, then breathed slowly in and out. "I'm sorry," she whispered, as though her reaction was something to apologize about.

"Don't be sorry," Luke told her. "It can't be easy for you," he said, and truly meant it. What he hadn't told her was the house she was to share with McTavish had been turned upside down, along with the small office he had in town. Hanson was looking for something, and apparently hadn't found it. He decided not to share this information with Mary, as she was already far too distressed. "Did you have a good sleep?" he asked, trying to change the subject.

Mary stared at him. "I did, but had a terrible fright to find you weren't here. I wasn't sure what to think."

His heart thudded. "I apologize," he said, and meant every word. If he hadn't left Peter to ensure her safety, who knew what could happen? Luke had a job to do, and that entailed giving an update to his superiors and receiving any new information. His responsibilities lay in ensuring Mary was safe, and trying to locate whatever it was Hanson was seeking.

Clearly, it was not only Mary in Hanson's sights. If she was his only target, why would he turn the house upside down when she wasn't there? His head ached trying to solve the puzzle. Only Luke hadn't come up with a solution. Whatever it was, he knew that's when Mary's safety would be assured.

If they could work that out, it might be easier to catch Rufus Hanson. Luke prayed for a quick resolution.

"Have something to eat, Luke. You looked stressed."

Luke stared into her face. He was supposed to be taking care of her, not the other way around. Luke shook his head. "Please don't worry yourself over me. I can take care of myself."

"I'm sure you can," she answered. "Let me fuss over you, please? It will give me something to do." She smiled briefly, and his heart fluttered. The last thing Luke wanted to do was fall in love with his charge. He was certain she didn't have feelings for him, so he needed to let it go. Besides, his job did not allow him to have a relationship. It was far too dangerous, and he was moved from place to place with a moment's notice.

Her words were almost pleading, and it broke Luke's heart. He understood what it was like to be locked up in a small room for days on end. Although they were both having to endure it, for Luke, the confinement was not so difficult, since he was able to leave their suite, even if that was only outside the door.

Or like today, when he was able to leave the train itself and make his enquiries.

Mary had no such luxuries available to her.

She wandered over to the refreshments trolley and poured him a mug of coffee. "Darn it, this coffee is cold," she said. "I suppose it would be, since it's been sitting there for quite a while," she muttered, more to herself than to him. She looked to be on the verge of tears again, and it pulled at Luke's heartstrings.

The entire situation was getting to her, and he didn't know what to do about it. The truth was, there was nothing he could do about it. They were stuck on the train until Hanson was in custody. "Lemonade is fine," he said. Not that Luke was a lemonade sort of guy, but the fact Mary was getting into a frenzy over something so trivial told him a lot.

She was not coping, but there was little he could do about it.

Chapter Thirteen

Mary felt as though she was on the edge of hysteria. The walls were closing in around her, and there was nothing she could do about it.

She wanted to scream, but the other passengers would hear, and that would not do at all. It would bring attention to her, which was totally the opposite of what they wanted. Her heart was pounding in her chest, and she was now lightheaded.

Glancing up at Luke, she noticed him watching her curiously. Had he realized? That she was…what? Hysterical? Or at least on the verge.

He stepped slowly toward her, and put his arms around her. Mary rested her head against his chest. She heard the steady beat of his heart—it almost matched hers. He didn't say a word, and neither did Mary. They simply stood there, each one comforting the other. At least that's the way she saw it.

How many times had Luke done this for the women he protected, she wondered. He'd probably married most of them, for the same reason he'd married her. She glanced up into his face. For the first time in days, he seemed relaxed, happy. She felt the same way.

Except Mary knew it wouldn't last. They couldn't stand there like this for the rest of the trip, although she would be sorely tempted.

His eyes stared down at her, and he smiled. "Feeling better?" he asked, then lifted his hand and caressed her cheek. Mary tilted her head until it rested in his hand. It felt good standing here with him this way.

Luke quickly pulled his hand away. As though it was burned. His smile became a frown, and his arms dropped to his sides. "We shouldn't be doing this," he whispered, his voice husky. Mary knew he was right, but at that moment, she didn't care.

"We're legally married. What harm could it do?" she asked quietly.

Instead of answering, Luke shook his head. He poured himself a glass of lemonade, then sat down in one of the comfortable chairs, leaving Mary standing by herself.

Rejection was the last thing she expected. But then again, so was being held in his arms.

~*~

It seemed like forever before the dinner trolley arrived. With it came two new books. Peter was a gem. He might be the railway detective, but he certainly knew how to keep Mary happy.

Holding the books, Luke looked them over. "*Portrait of a Lady*," he said, eyebrows raised. "And *Uncle Tom's Cabin*. That's an interesting assortment." He handed them to her, then rolled the trolley further into the room.

Mary sighed. Luke was right, you couldn't get two totally different books. At least they would keep her occupied for a while. She hated doing nothing, always had. It was one of the things she enjoyed about working at the mercantile. There was always something to do. A shelf to be tidied or refilled, accounts to be written up, customers to serve. Her days went fast, and she enjoyed her job thoroughly.

Except now she didn't have a job. Donald insisted she resign before they married, and so she did. Mary worked right up until the day before their wedding. It was a sad day for her. Not only did she worry how she would fill her days, but her independence was suddenly gone.

When she told Donald how she felt, he was furious. He reiterated his words the last time she'd brought it up—*no wife of mine will work*, he'd said, explaining he made more than enough for both of them. Foolishly, Mary hadn't looked ahead to what else might change after her marriage.

Looking back, she now understood their marriage would not have been a good one. If Donald hadn't been murdered, what else would he have wanted to change? She couldn't help but wonder, especially given she was now being pursued by Donald's killer.

"Everything alright?" Luke asked as she sat at the table.

His words were enough to bring her back to reality. "I was just thinking," she said. "If Donald was still alive, what I would be doing now."

Luke stared at her for about thirty seconds. Did that mean he was pondering the question too? "For starters, you would be right here on the train. Except you would be free to move about. But then again, Hanson may have been trying to find your husband. Everyone on the train would be in danger then."

Mary knew he was right. Donald McTavish had proven himself to be selfish and uncaring. As much as his sudden death had been a shock, it probably happened that way for the best. If they'd got beyond the courthouse, how many innocent bystanders would have become collateral damage?

Several people were on the boardwalk nearby, and of course, Mary stood by his side—her arm hooked through Donald's. She'd had no idea what happened until his arm slid out from hers when he slumped to the ground.

The very thought of it had her head spinning. Mary knew she had to focus on the task at hand. Dinner. Luke removed the covers from their food, and the aroma was delicious. For tonight, she had ordered roasted duck. Plum sauce accompanied the duck, and was served in an elegant gravy boat.

"You ordered the duck, too," Mary noted. "You don't have to order the same as me." She shrugged her shoulders, then poured herself a cup of tea. Luke had coffee. Strong and black.

"I happen to like duck," he said in a wounded voice.

It made Mary laugh. "Then I guess that's alright," she said, trying unsuccessfully to quell her laughter.

She reached across the table for his hand, and they said grace, then began to eat.

The more Mary got to know Luke, the more she liked him. What she would do when they parted ways, she didn't know. She had become very accustomed to his presence, and couldn't imagine life without him.

Chapter Fourteen

The train moved forward with a jolt. As much as he should deny it, Luke was quite pleased when Mary landed in his arms.

Supper was over, and Mary had announced she was going to bed. They stood at almost the same moment, then the train began to move. Unfortunately, or perhaps it was fortunate for Luke, they'd been catapulted together as they moved from their stable and thankfully peaceful environment at Helena station.

Luke's arms automatically reached out to stop her from falling, and Mary didn't complain. "Thank you," she said quietly, glancing up at him.

It was then she did something unexpected. Mary licked her lips, then went up on her toes and kissed him.

Stunned. That's what Luke was in that moment. Never had he believed Mary would kiss him. Not for any reason. Not that Luke was complaining. He enjoyed her lips on his, and wished it could last forever.

It wasn't to be.

Bringing herself back to her normal height, Mary rested her head on his chest. Should he say something? Admonish her behavior? Luke knew he should—Mary had stepped over the line of their professional relationship and made it more personal. If he was honest with himself, Luke would have kissed her long ago, only his ethics stopped him from doing so.

His hand went up and caressed her cheek, and instead of pushing it away, Mary covered his hand with hers. Was she ensuring Luke didn't move his hand away? He would likely never know.

"I'm not sorry," she said firmly, and it was all he could do not to laugh. This was the side of Mary he enjoyed the most. The one that was defiant, and said the most inappropriate things at times. She said what was on her mind, not caring what anyone else thought.

Luke could see McTavish enjoying her antics as well, but he would surely have become tired of them after a while. Luke would never tire of Mary's open and honest words. She made him smile at the worst of times, and had him laughing out loud at the best times.

His arms tightened around her, and although he knew he shouldn't, Luke wanted to kiss her. This time, he would be the one to instigate. He leaned down, his heart pounding, and gently lifted her chin with his fingers.

She glanced up at him with her puppy brown eyes, almost pleading Luke to hurry up. "Are you sure this is what you want?" he asked, waiting for her answer. Consent was important to him, as he was certain it would be to his wife.

His wife.

What had he been thinking when he married her? Even if it was to be temporary, it was probably the stupidest thing he'd even done. Not that he could admit it to Mary, but he didn't want an annulment when all of this was over.

He had fallen for her, and fallen hard. Their close proximity probably didn't help, but Luke knew it was more than that. His heart would shatter into pieces when this was over, and they were no longer married. He already knew it, so why was he trying to kiss her?

Before he could think, Mary put her arms around his neck and pulled Luke closer. Then she kissed him. She leaned back after a few moments and stared into his face. "What are you waiting for?" she asked, a smile on her face.

At that moment, Luke realized he was forever lost. His heart belonged to Mary Flanagan, his pretend wife, who he dearly wanted to have as his real wife.

"I can't do this," Luke said, knowing he should have put a stop to it earlier. "I am here to protect you, not to take advantage."

"Take advantage?" Mary said so quietly he almost missed it. "If me kissing you first is taking advantage, then so be it," she said between clenched teeth.

Mary pulled out of his arms, and Luke's heart thudded. As much as he wanted Mary at this very moment, he had to acknowledge it wasn't the best move. "There's an unwritten rule about being a protector—we are not meant to have a relationship with the person we're looking out for."

He watched as fury made its way into her face. Mary pursed her lips, and her cheeks turned a bright red color. "It's not like I don't want to kiss you," he said firmly. "There's a reason for the rule," he said urgently. "If we get too close, it's much more difficult to be detached if something goes awry."

Tapping her foot did nothing to make Luke feel better. Then Mary's hands went to her hips. He almost expected to see smoke coming out of her ears. The sight before him was both serious and funny.

"Rules are meant to be broken," Mary said, then turned away from him. "I'm going to bed," she said gruffly, then stormed into the small bathroom in their suite.

Luke's heart shattered. He knew the rules, and was fully aware of what could happen if he let himself get too close. Never before had he protected someone while they were both stuck in the one room, and especially sharing the same bed.

The temptation was there, but he would not cross the line. Except Luke knew he had already done that, simply by holding Mary in his arms.

Luke was aching all over. Spending the entire night in what was supposed to be a comfortable chair, really wasn't that comfortable. He was certain Mary would reject him if he tried to join her on the bed.

Not that he slept under the covers—he always laid on the top. He was fully clothed, with his gun under the pillow for easy access. Except she was so mad with him last night, he didn't want to risk Mary's wrath. They still had to spend time together until she was safe. That could be mere days, or it might be far longer.

He stood and stretched himself out, glancing across at the bed as he did so. Mary was still sound asleep. It had taken Luke a long time to settle into sleep. Hours, in fact, and that was due to their disagreement.

Trouble was, Luke had done what he knew to be right. Mary did not like it one bit, but he had to do what he believed to be right for both of them. He only wished he'd kept his distance from the get-go. Perhaps at the next stop he should request a replacement. Except that would be difficult given they were married. What his superiors would say about that, Luke didn't know.

Except Luke had to admit he did know. They would be furious. He had been trained to keep his distance, and until now, he'd done exactly that.

Beyond the rules, Luke knew staying was the right thing to do. Especially for Mary.

Chapter Fifteen

Mary heard movement in the room, and assumed it was Luke. He'd not come to lie next to her last night, and that hurt. In hindsight, she privately acknowledged she'd done the wrong thing.

Luke was right. He had to keep his distance. Only her feelings for him were growing by the day. She was also becoming too dependent on him being with her during her waking hours. It was a difficult pill to swallow, but Mary knew it was the truth.

Before Donald came along and disrupted her relatively quiet life, she was far more independent than most women she knew. Mary made all her own decisions, earned her own money, and lived in the house she grew up in.

Her parents were long gone, more's the pity, and she had no wish to leave her childhood home. Donald insisted she sell it, but Mary hadn't yet done so. She knew now she wouldn't.

A slight groan came from Luke as he stood and stretched himself out. It was his own fault. She didn't make him sleep in the chair, although he probably thought she'd want him too. At the time she did, but now Mary felt bad. Pretending she was still asleep seemed childish, but she was still annoyed about last night. She'd shown her hand to Luke, and he'd rejected her.

She rolled over and opened her eyes, letting him know she was awake. Luke glanced across at her, and his expression softened. How could she stay mad at him when he clearly brightened up on seeing her awake? The truth was, she couldn't. "Good morning," Mary said, her voice still husky from sleep. At least that was the excuse she gave herself.

At first he seemed wary, then he sat on the edge of the bed and smiled. "Good morning," he said quietly, a fragment of caution in his voice.

Did Luke think she would hold his actions against him for the rest of their time together? That she would waste those precious moments they did have left? Mary had resigned herself to the reality of it all—they needed to keep their distance. She admitted they must keep things on a professional level, for both their sakes.

"Breakfast will arrive soon," Luke said, then headed into the bathroom. When he returned, his previously mussed up hair was wet and perfectly in place. Mary couldn't believe it had her heart racing. Hadn't she already resolved to keep her distance?

If only her body cooperated, it would be far easier to stick to the plan.

There was a knock at the door, and a voice telling them breakfast had arrived. Mary hurried into the bathroom while Luke answered the door. As she did so, Mary had a feeling of foreboding come over her.

She couldn't explain why she felt that way as a shiver went down her spine. Did that mean something bad was about to happen? Mary hoped it wasn't true. Opening the door tentatively, she warily glanced into their suite. Luke was rolling the trolley next to the table. He wouldn't be doing that if something awful had happened.

What that something awful was, she had no idea. She released a huge sigh of relief, then headed toward the table.

Luke glanced at her curiously. "Is something wrong?" he asked.

"Quite the contrary," Mary said. "I had a bad feeling. It was like someone walked over my grave." She shuddered then. Saying it out loud made it seem even worse.

Luke laughed. "As you can see, all is well. Breakfast has arrived, so it's time to sit down and eat."

Mary did just that—sitting down and reaching for the pot of tea. It was really all she needed, but Luke insisted she keep her strength up. He had reiterated several times they simply didn't know when they would need it.

Luke placed Mary's breakfast in front of her. She leaned in and breathed in the enticing smell. She'd ordered pancakes with stewed apples for today. Not exactly a breakfast meal, but it was something she enjoyed.

She glanced across at Luke's plate. He had bacon and eggs with sausages and toast on the side. The meal was huge, and although it looked like a lot to Mary, she knew Luke would get through it all. He'd had that most days and finished the lot.

He lifted his coffee and sipped the hot beverage, watching Mary over the top of his mug. Luke enjoyed his coffee as much as Mary enjoyed her tea.

They said grace, then began to eat. Neither said another word until their meal was over.

~*~

"Do you think I'll ever be safe?" Mary asked as they sat quietly in the comfortable chairs.

Luke turned to face her. "I certainly hope so," he said gently. "I would like to hope we'll have Hanson in custody sooner than later. You need to be safe," he said.

Mary looked at him quizzically. It sounded as though his voice was breaking on his last words. "Luke?" she asked, wondering what that was about.

He turned his head away, giving her even more reason to wonder. "It's nothing," he said, but Mary knew his words to be untrue.

Her heart thudded. It made her wonder if he felt the same way she did, but as they'd already discussed, he had to keep his distance. It was the last thing Mary wanted, but she would comply with his wishes.

At least for now.

The knock at the door startled her. She retreated into the bathroom, as Luke demanded each time someone came to the door.

"It's the railway detective," she heard moments before she closed the bathroom door. Knowing it was Peter gave her pause, and Mary was about to go back out. Except it didn't sound like Peter's voice. Nor did he ever address himself as the railway detective when he came to their door.

Her heart thudded.

The next thing Mary heard was Luke yelling at whoever stood outside their suite. It certainly wasn't Peter.

Another voice was added to the mix, and this time she did recognize Peter's voice. She cowered in the corner of the bathroom, not sure what to do. She was certain Luke would want her to stay right where she was, and not cause him additional stress.

Scuffling was combined with yelling, until suddenly all was quiet. She expected to hear gunshots any moment, and that was her biggest fear. She couldn't lose Luke. She just couldn't. She loved him too much for that.

Her thoughts made her stop and think. Mary knew she'd become very fond of her protector, but not once had she admitted the truth to herself. She was deeply in love with him.

Luke would brush her feelings aside, and tell her it's all due to circumstances, she was certain he would. But Mary knew her own heart. The question was, did Luke know his?

Despite everything going on around her, Mary's thoughts had turned to Luke. Not to herself or her own welfare, but to Luke and whether or not he had been injured or killed during the scuffle.

Mary was shaking, and despite trying to stop, she couldn't. Her legs were like jelly, and she couldn't find the strength to stand up and learn the truth.

The door flew open, and her heart seemed to stop. Everything happened in slow motion. Glancing up,

Luke stood in front of her, then stooped down and helped Mary to her feet. Tears of relief filled her eyes and flooded her cheeks. "I...I thought you were dead," she whispered, moments before Luke pulled her close against him.

"I am very much alive," he said, then lifted her chin with his fingers and kissed her thoroughly.

When he lifted his head, Mary slumped against him, her tears saturating his shirt. "What happened?" she asked. "Was it Hanson?"

Luke shook his head. "Not Hanson, but one of his stooges. He is now locked up, the worse for wear."

Mary read between the lines—Hanson was still out there, and still wanted her dead. Would she ever be safe again?

Luke could not protect her forever. Even if that was what she truly wanted.

Chapter Sixteen

Before he even opened the door, Luke knew it was not Peter Jameson on the other side. For one, Peter didn't identify himself as *railway detective*. He always used his name. Second, Peter had a very distinctive voice, and this person didn't have that.

Gun in hand, he slowly opened the door, not knowing what or who he would encounter on the other side. The moment he clapped eyes on the imposter, Luke knew he was in trouble. This man was huge, not only in height, but he was big and solid. Despite his training, Luke knew he couldn't tackle this man alone.

Thankfully, Peter, the real railway detective, happened to be in the vicinity of the suite, and helped tackle the man to the ground before he had a chance to reach for his gun.

The entire time, Luke was sorely aware Mary would be alone and feeling terrified. There was nothing he could do about it. Between them, Luke and Peter managed to overcome the man and Peter handcuffed him.

He hated the thought of going into the bathroom, knowing full well Mary would be absolutely petrified.

She still shook when he pulled her close, but she was safe. For now, anyway. Not that he intended to tell Mary, but it was fairly obvious, at least to Luke, that Hanson had worked out where she was. He had to get her out of here.

Her life depended on it.

"Peter will be back shortly. If you'd rather he didn't, tell me now," Luke said. He felt her relax a little more against him.

"Let me clean up before he comes," she whispered. Luke understood she was referring to the redness of her face, even though Mary hadn't mentioned it.

"Of course," he said, reluctant to take his arms from around her. Doing his job properly meant not holding her like this. And it definitely meant he wasn't to kiss her. Except he wanted to do both— forever more.

He mentally shook himself. He had more important things to worry about, and couldn't afford to think about loving Mary. It was the entire reason the rule about not getting personal was put in place.

It was almost as though his superiors knew this could be a possibility.

Federal Marshals must not form a personal relationship with the clients they are to protect.

He even had the words in the handbook memorized. Why, then, hadn't he heeded them? Luke knew exactly why—Mary was special. He might have married her to stop gossip and protect her reputation, but almost from the moment they met, he knew she was special.

It was even more reason not to marry her, and not get close. He was a fool for not heeding the rules.

"I'll leave you to do whatever it is you have to do," Luke said, then closed the bathroom door behind him. He felt like a jerk doing it, especially while she still trembled, but he needed to talk with Peter.

Only moments later, Peter called through the door as he knocked. "I bring peace offerings," he called.

The moment the door was ajar, Peter rolled the refreshments trolley inside. "The prisoner is locked up and secure. I am concerned..." he began.

Luke nodded. "I agree—we need to get Mary off this train."

Mary opened the door at the wrong time. Luke had to assume she heard every word. "Oh!" she said, her voice full of surprise. "I guess that means Rufus Hanson knows where I am."

"He does," Peter said firmly. "The fact one of his men infiltrated the train has proven it. I'm sorry," he said, and sounded very genuine. "Next stop is soon after lunch. Get your belongings together, and I'll ensure they get to the hotel in town."

"I can't take Mary out in the open air," Luke protested, and rightly so. "Do you have any ideas?"

"I do," Peter said firmly. "I'm certain it will work. We get fresh linen at the next stop. We hide her in the trolley, and…"

"Hmmm," Mary said. She didn't sound very convinced. "You want me to hide underneath dirty linen?" She sounded incredulous.

"It won't be dirty. I'll ensure it's clean." Peter seemed very confident. Besides, Luke didn't have a better idea.

"Let's do it," Luke said, although he had some reservations, but it was the only idea they had at this point in time.

Luke glanced across the room to where Mary sat on one of the chairs. She didn't look at all happy, but it was just too bad. Their options were limited.

As the train came to a halt, Peter Jameson entered the suite where Mary sat waiting for the inevitable. Luke felt really bad about shoving her into the linen trolley. Although they would be careful getting her in there.

She sat in the chair, taking deep breaths. Until now, she had held it together pretty well. Knowing she would be out in the open between the train and the hotel, Mary was understandably worried. Hanson didn't know either Peter or Luke, and they would be nearby. It would simply look as though they were headed to the hotel.

The suite had been cleared of all Luke and Mary's belongings, and nothing was left to identify them having been there.

Luke walked over to her as the door closed behind Peter. "Are you ready?" he asked, despite knowing she was anxious about the transfer. One of the workers would push Mary to safety, but did not know Mary would be inside the trolley.

Mary finally stood. She nodded, but Luke instinctively knew she was not at all happy. She really was a trooper. Mary had gone along with everything that had been thrown at her, even if she didn't agree with doing it.

Luke held Mary close, and whispered in her ear. "I'll be right behind you, as will Peter. You will get jostled about somewhat as the trolley is removed from the train." He heard her gasp. "Whatever you do, do not pop your head up to see what is going on. You will be a sitting duck." He held her a little closer, and desperately wanted to kiss her. Luke knew he mustn't. Instead, he kissed her forehead.

Peter helped Luke tuck her underneath the sheets and other linen. "I'll see you outside," Peter told them as the housemaid arrived. Peter assured Luke she knew nothing except she had to collect this trolley and take it straight to where the other soiled linen was removed from the train.

Luke watched from the doorway as Mary was taken out of his sight. It pained him to leave her like this, but it was the only way to ensure her safety. They would soon be reunited, but that didn't stop his heart from twisting in pain.

Chapter Seventeen

Mary's heart pounded so hard she could hear it in her head. Everything around her was muffled, and she was hidden underneath a bevy of sheets and towels. At first she worried she wouldn't be able to breathe, but the two men assured her she would be able to breathe just fine.

What she mustn't do is panic, they told her. If she panicked, she might hyperventilate, and that, in turn, would hinder her breathing.

The trolley suddenly moved, and Mary put a fist to her mouth to stop herself from making even the tiniest sound. It could, and probably would, be the difference between life and death. She couldn't risk even the slightest noise that alerted anyone standing nearby there was a person in that trolley. She had been tucked in well, to camouflage her presence, with piles of towels and linen covering her completely. With sides of white linen, her brightly colored clothes would otherwise be seen through the thin sides. Donald had insisted on buying her a whole new wardrobe of clothes. Mary didn't get to choose any of them.

It was then she realized he was not a good match for her—he'd become manipulative even before they married. By then, it was too late to change her mind. Donald had made all the arrangements, and spent a lot of money on her, including their honeymoon on the train. She'd convinced herself he wouldn't be that way once they married.

She never had the chance to find out, since he was murdered mere minutes after they married.

Mary felt another bump, this time a much bigger one. The trolley was being lifted down from the train onto the platform, she was certain. Peter had ensured she knew what to expect, and not to scream or make a sound.

This was their only chance to get her off the train unnoticed. She closed her eyes and tried to breathe normally. She silently prayed for her safe extradition to the hotel where the linen from the Pullman car was cleaned and returned. Knowing both Peter and Luke weren't far away gave her some reassurance. At least for now.

It wasn't long before Mary heard muffled voices all around her. She had to stay put, despite the terror of it all. She had no way of knowing who was nearby, and whether Rufus Hanson was amongst them.

Luke assured her the transfer wouldn't take long, and he would let her know when it was safe to come out.

Her heart thudded, and she felt like she might pass out, but Mary was not a wilting flower. Instead, she was a strong woman in charge of her own fate. She would be fine. She would survive. She would…

Suddenly, the linen was pulled away and Luke stood over her. He reached down and gently lifted her out. "We did it," he whispered. "We got you out."

Her eyes filled with tears, and Mary leaned into her fake husband. The man she wanted to spend the rest of her life with.

Luke held Mary tighter than he ever had before. She was shaking, but so was he. Did that mean Luke genuinely cared for her? Mary didn't know what to think. With her arms around his waist, all she wanted to do was kiss him, but being held like this by the man she loved worked equally well.

Until now, Mary had mostly kept her eyes tightly closed, wanting to block out the rest of the world. She didn't even know where she was, but guessed probably in their hotel room. Otherwise, she would be seen by anyone who wandered into the hotel.

Now, though, she decided to open them. She should familiarize herself with their surroundings. Who knew what might happen and they needed to get away? Her eyes fluttered open, and the first thing she saw was Luke's shirt and jacket. And the edge of his gun and holster. It sent a shiver down her spine.

Mary closed her eyes again, trying to block out the vision, the reality of her situation. She turned her head to face the other side. There was no gun there. At least she presumed there wasn't. Violence had never been a part of her life, and now that it was, it scared her half to death.

Luke's hand caressed her cheek. "It's alright," he told her in a whispered voice. "It's only you and me here. We're in our hotel room."

Opening her eyes slowly, Mary didn't want to move out of his embrace. She was happy and content right where she was. Mary's breath left her in a whoosh. She was safe. At least for now. "What about Hanson?" As much as she didn't want to know, Mary needed to know the truth.

Luke loosened his grip on her. "There's no sign of him. Peter is looking, but he'll keep well hidden. Until the coward is ready to show himself."

"Then what?" Mary said quietly.

A hand began to roam around her back, making Mary feel more content than previously. "That will depend on Hanson. If he comes quietly, it will be better for all concerned."

Mary was reading between the lines. They both knew it was highly unlikely that Hanson would give himself up. From the little she knew about the outlaw, even if he was cornered, he would fight to the end.

"Am I to presume I cannot leave this room?" Mary asked, her voice giving away her discontent at the idea.

"It's too dangerous. Not knowing whether Hanson is loitering somewhere close means you must stay hidden. You will have every possible luxury here. Even a hot bath, if that's what you want."

A hot bath sounded like pure indulgence, and Mary would love that. Provided they could hide her identity. Would that even be possible? "It does sound wonderful."

When Luke's arms dropped from around her, Mary felt empty. She knew he wouldn't be with her much longer. The moment they caught Rufus Hanson, she would be alone. She couldn't bear the thought, but knew it was inevitable. Her heart skipped a beat simply thinking about it. "Our bags will arrive shortly, and we might as well prepare for the long haul. We could be here for weeks."

"Weeks? Surely not." But then again, what else did she have to do? Donald forced her to give up her job, although she did have the ranch and farmhouse she inherited from her parents. Mary would have to find another job or beg for her old job back. Provided it hadn't already been filled, that was. "I don't think I can stand being locked up for that long." She glanced about. "At least this room is much bigger than our suite on the train."

Luke followed her gaze. "It definitely is. That's not necessarily good from a protection point of view, but we will make do."

Mary sighed. If she had to be locked up with someone, she was glad it was Luke. When it came time to part ways, she wasn't sure how she would cope. Right now, her heart was filled with love. When their marriage was annulled, it would be hollow like a rotting tree trunk. It wasn't what she wanted, and Mary wasn't sure she would ever get over Luke Flanagan, her pretend husband.

Chapter Eighteen

With each passing day, Luke became more enamored with Mary. As much as he tried to keep his distance, it simply didn't work. She was special, he'd known it from the moment they met. What he would do when all of this was over, he wasn't sure.

Luke shook himself mentally. It would be totally up to Mary what she wanted to do. Right now, she was attached to him because of her current circumstances. It was to be expected.

"I'll arrange that hot bath," he said. "Thankfully, there's hot running water here."

"It's a high-class hotel, then?" Mary said.

Luke laughed. "It's the only hotel in town. They get a lot of tourists, so ensure they are happy."

Mary wandered around the room, familiarizing herself with the layout. It really was quite large. The main room held a double bed, two armchairs, a small table and two chairs. There was also a private bathroom that held a bath, a water closet and handbasin. Since it had full plumbing, including hot water, Luke didn't have to worry about Mary being seen.

There was a small closet that would hold their clothing. "We will be here for a while," Luke said. "Feel free to unpack whenever you're ready."

Mary went to her suitcase and sorted through her clothing. She hung her gowns in the closet, and added her undergarments to a drawer. "I'm getting low on clothes. Do they have laundry facilities here?" With the suitcase empty, she turned to her carpetbag. It held only one change of clothes, and was more for emergencies than anything.

"I believe they do," Luke said, then watched her curiously. "What do you have there?" he asked, moving closer to where Mary stood. He leaned in, trying to get a better look in the carpetbag.

"My unmentionables," Mary said, clearly annoyed at him.

"Not those. I can see something sticking out from the base of the bag." Luke's heart pounded. Surely it wasn't what he thought it was.

His head was spinning, and Luke was keen to have a closer look. He was disturbed by a knock at the door. "It's Peter Jameson," the voice called through the door. Luke relaxed. If Hanson discovered where Mary was hidden, he would definitely come after her.

Luke opened the door, still as vigilant as ever, checking the hallways as he let Peter inside. "I was moments away from checking Mary's carpetbag," he told the railway detective. The pair stepped forward.

Mary snatched up her undergarments and fled into the closet to finish unpacking.

Luke barely withheld a grin. Now empty of clothes, he took the carpetbag over to the table, and tried unsuccessfully to pull out whatever had been concealed. "Did you pack this bag yourself, Mary?" Luke asked, convinced he already knew the answer.

Mary turned to stare at him. "No, I didn't," she said, then sighed. "Donald insisted on buying new clothes for me, along with the carpetbag. When I retrieved it at the house, I discovered he'd already packed the bag."

There was a pocket at the side, and Luke pulled out the packet it held. "This must be for you," he told Mary. "It's gift wrapped. I want you to open it here. Or I can do it if you'd rather."

She frowned. "Should I be worried?" she asked, stepping away from the package Luke held out to her?"

"I doubt it," Luke said. "There's a note attached. It appears to be a wedding gift."

Mary stepped forward again and read the note. "It says, Happy Wedding Day, Donald." Her voice was breaking up the more she read. Mary ripped open the decorated paper to find a vanity set inside. Luke watched as she lifted each piece and inspected it. It consisted of a hairbrush, clothes brush, mirror, powder bowl, and a trinket tray.

"It's a truly beautiful gift for any lady." As he spoke the words, Luke noticed the tears in her eyes.

"Do you think Donald would have been a…a good husband?" Mary seemed genuinely interested.

Luke's heart thudded. How could she think Donald McTavish, a notorious criminal, would have made a good husband? "I doubt it," he said, since she clearly wanted an answer.

Mary nodded, then wandered back to the closet, leaving the men to retrieve whatever had been concealed at the bottom of Mary's carpetbag.

"I believe we'll have to cut this open," Luke said, then pulled out a pocket knife. "It comes in handy sometimes," he explained, when Peter stared at the weapon Luke held.

"Why would McTavish have put a false bottom in Mary's carpetbag? It would mean he was risking his wife possibly witnessing whatever it was he had to do with the contents."

As much as Peter had a good point, Luke believed Donald McTavish was capable of anything.

Luke put the knife back in his pocket. "Perhaps this is not a good choice," he said. "I don't want to damage what could be crucial evidence." The two men then struggled to pull out what they believed was a false base in the bag. When it finally gave way, they couldn't believe their eyes.

~*~

Mary entered the room at the same time Peter was about to leave. "I'll be back later," Peter said moments before he opened the door.

What he didn't mention, was the task Luke had set him. It wouldn't take long to do, but it may take time to get a response.

"Would you like some refreshments?" Luke asked, trying to distract Mary from asking questions. The moment she noticed her carpetbag had been destroyed, he was certain her curiosity would get the better of her.

"I am rather parched," she said, glancing at the bag. "What have you done?" she asked accusingly. "That bag was brand new. Donald bought it only days before we were to marry." She crossed her arms and tapped her foot, no doubt waiting for an answer.

Luke sighed. He knew this would be an issue, but he couldn't risk the bag leaving the room. What they found was far too precious. "Don't you worry your pretty little head about it," he said as he stepped toward her. Instead of pacifying Mary, it only served to make her angry.

"I'm not an idiot!" she hissed, then headed into the bathroom.

It wasn't long before Luke heard running water. Perhaps it wasn't a bad thing—a hot bath would help calm his wife, and keep her distracted for a while. The last thing he wanted was for Mary to get caught up in Donald's criminal activities, even though her dead husband had given her no choice. She'd been entrenched in them, purely by the man marrying her.

It was then Luke decided Donald McTavish didn't have any feelings at all for Mary—he'd used her to conceal his activities. He'd given no thought to the fact Rufus Hanson would come after him, and in turn, Mary, for the information contained in that bag.

He wondered if McTavish would have protected her if Hanson had cornered them, but quickly decided he would only look out for himself. It was typical of the criminal types he'd come across during his years as a marshal.

The water stopped running, taking his mind to places he knew it shouldn't go. Mary would be undressing to climb into the bath. If they were truly married, he could wash her back. In the process of doing that, he would likely kiss her neck.

Except they weren't really married. Their marriage was a farce. Despite his assurance they would annul the marriage once the danger was over, Luke no longer wanted an annulment. He was falling more in love with Mary by the day.

He shook his head, trying to clear away forbidden thoughts. Luke knew it wasn't an option to stay married. His job took him all over the place, which meant he was rarely home. What sort of marriage would that be? It certainly wouldn't be good for Mary.

Besides, she was probably more than keen to be released from their wedding vows. Two marriages in one day, and neither one was for love.

If he knew anything about Mary, marriage was important to her, and love would have to be at the core of it.

Chapter Nineteen

Mary climbed into the hot bath. The fragrant oils supplied by the hotel made the bath even more enticing. She'd used lavender—Mary's favorite fragrance.

She was so angry with Luke right now, and hoped the soaking would make her feel better. The entire scenario she'd found herself in was upsetting. But to be treated like a fool was infuriating. Mary was certain Luke was trying to protect her from whatever he'd found, but that wasn't the point. Telling her *not to worry her pretty little head about it* was demeaning. It gave the impression he thought she was an idiot. It certainly made her feel that way.

Except Mary knew Luke didn't think of her that way, she was sure. What he and Peter Jameson were planning, she may never know. Instead of fretting about the situation, Mary brought the face cloth to her face. It was infused with lavender oil since it had been soaking in the bath water.

The fragrance was alluring, and it was also relaxing. It was one of the reasons Mary had chosen lavender. She leaned her head back onto the edge of the bath and closed her eyes. It was beyond relaxing, it was comforting. It was also exactly what she needed.

The past week or so had stressed her beyond normal limits. Mary had no idea what would happen from one day to the next, let alone each moment.

Her nerves were on edge, and Mary knew it was the reason she'd lost her temper with Luke. Doing so was very much out of character for her, and Mary felt remorseful at becoming so angry. Especially when she knew Luke was trying to protect her.

"Mary," Luke called through the door. "Are you alright?"

Her eyes flew open. "Don't come in!" she shouted. "I'm…I'm…" She didn't want to say the word out loud. Telling Luke she was stark naked seemed wrong, even if he was legally her husband.

"I won't, I promise," he said. "I merely wanted to make sure you hadn't drowned. You've been in there for a long time."

A long time? It didn't seem very long to her. "How long?" Mary asked, bringing herself to a sitting position.

She heard Luke laughing. "Almost thirty minutes," he told her, much to Mary's shock.

In that case, she should get out of the bath. Running her hands through the water, the proof was there—it was lukewarm. Glancing around, Mary discovered a problem. Her heart thudded. "Luke," she called through the door. "There are no towels in here." The last thing she wanted was for him to come into the bathroom and see her naked, but what choice did she have? She was so angry when she went there, she hadn't given towels a thought.

Mary heard what she thought was Luke chuckling. He might think it funny, but she certainly did not.

"I'm coming in," he called, then opened the door.

Mary's heart thudded. Even as a married woman, she didn't want her husband to see her naked. Luke, being the true gentleman he was, held out the towel for her, his eyes tightly closed. "Can you reach it?" he asked, not moving far inside the room.

Standing in the bath, which was still full of water, she snatched the towel out of his hand. "Oh!" Mary squealed, as she began to fall. She hadn't thought about the slippery base. Luke's eyes flew open, and he stepped forward to help.

Mary was devastated. No man had ever seen her naked. Until today.

Luke quickly wrapped her in the towel and lifted her out of the water. "I didn't look, I promise," he said, then quickly retreated, leaving Mary alone to dry off.

She wasn't sure she would ever recover from the embarrassment.

~*~

Mary didn't know which way to look when she finally exited from the bathroom. She was certain Luke would never look at her the same way again. The same was true for herself. She was overcome with embarrassment, and wondered how Luke was feeling right now.

As she entered the main part of the suite, she looked everywhere except at Luke. He sat at the table, reading the newspaper. He didn't so much as glance at her when Mary entered the room. She felt the heat rolling up her cheeks, and wanted to melt into the ground. Unfortunately, they were stuck there. Together. For goodness knew how long.

"How are you feeling now?" Luke asked.

Did he mean after their unfortunate encounter, or was he referring to her outburst which prompted her to storm out of the room? Either way, Mary was not proud of herself. Her short temper caused one event, and her lack of forethought caused the other. She should have realized the towels would be on the end of the bed. Wasn't that how most hotels worked? Not that she'd visited many in her life, but those she had? It was exactly what they'd all done.

Mary glanced in his direction. Luke didn't seem too fussed about their bathroom mishap. More likely, it was the highlight of his day. Or week. Or month. Mary assumed it wouldn't happen very often, so would be something out of the ordinary.

It certainly was for her. "About before…" she began, but he interrupted her.

"No need to apologize," he said.

His words got her back up. "Apologize?" Her voice rose in a most unladylike fashion. "I have nothing to apologize for!" she shouted, trying without success to keep the screeching sound to a minimum.

Instead of answering, Luke laughed. Not chuckled, or even smiled. He laughed out loud, and was clearly enjoying himself.

"Men!" she shouted, then sat in one of the comfortable chairs.

The laughing stopped at the very moment there was a knock on the door. He indicated for Mary to go into the closet, out of sight. "It's the railway detective," the voice said through the door. But to Mary, it didn't sound like Peter. Nor did he ever address himself that way.

"Get in that closet now," Luke demanded as he reached for his gun.

Her heart pounded, and not in a good way.

Chapter Twenty

The moment he heard the words through the door, Luke knew something was amiss. Peter didn't address himself that way, and besides, he was downtown, undertaking a task for Luke. Hopefully, back-up would arrive sooner than later.

Right now, though, he needed to try and stall whoever was on the other side of the door. Luke's guess was Rufus Hanson or someone from his gang. Perhaps even both. The thought of being outnumbered didn't appeal to Luke, and he glanced behind him to check out the windows. Peter had chosen this room because it was upstairs, and couldn't be entered from outside.

As much as it stopped others getting inside, it also meant he and Mary couldn't climb outside. There weren't a lot of options—they needed to stay and fight. The very thought of Mary being in such a precarious position sent a shudder through him, and Luke held tight to his gun.

He decided not to answer, hoping perhaps whomever stood on the other side would leave. Except he knew it wouldn't happen, as they would surely have heard him talking to Mary a short time ago. Luke glanced toward the closet, ensuring Mary was still inside. He'd stowed the now destroyed carpetbag in there, which meant if they got past him, Mary would be in a direct line of gunfire.

His heart pounded. In that moment, he understood why it was imperative for agents not to become attached to clients. His job was to protect Mary at all costs. And that's exactly what he would do. If something should go awry and she was in imminent danger, his feelings toward her may color his actions.

It was a dilemma he couldn't afford to have.

"I know Mrs. McTavish is in there," the voice said, confirming Luke's earlier suspicions. Rufus Hanson had somehow located Mary. It had to be a lucky guess. There was no other way he could find her.

Or perhaps he was going from room to room doing this same thing. Luke could only hope so. He stood to the side, ensuring he was not putting himself in danger. Not knowing who was there, and what weapons, if any, they had made him more than a little nervous.

"I can give them what they want," Mary said quietly, causing Luke to spin around to face her.

"Get inside that closet," he spat. Pursing her lips, Mary stood firm. "You don't even know what he wants," Luke whispered. "Please, you're making it harder."

She brushed back her hair with a shaking hand. It was then Luke realized Mary was as worried as he was.

"There's no Mrs. McTavish here," he called back. "You've got the wrong room."

Suddenly, there was silence. Did that mean they'd left? Or were they pretending to leave, hoping Luke would open the door to check. And how did they know about Peter? Perhaps he was involved after all, but Luke doubted it.

Peter had been an ally from the very beginning. If he was part of the Hanson gang, he could have eliminated them both the moment they arrived on the train. And yet he didn't.

It wouldn't be hard to find out who Peter was, Luke realized. Since he called here every time the train came through. All Hanson would have to do is ask one of the staff who he was.

Luke sighed. This was getting more complicated by the minute.

Sitting impatiently on the edge of the bed, Luke prayed Hanson had given up. And yet, he would put nothing past the hardened criminal. He'd already murdered Douglas McTavish, and there was nothing stopping him from killing Mary.

Except for Luke himself.

He had no intention of letting Hanson close enough to Mary that he would get a shot off. Luke would do whatever it took to keep him away. Even if that meant the outlaw was carried out in a body bag. Luke had dealt with his sort before. They were all about the money. Douglas McTavish made the mistake of flouting his riches, instead of keeping a low profile.

It appeared McTavish had threatened Hanson with exposure, and decided to put an end to the man. The evidence in that carpetbag would keep Hanson behind bars for a very long time.

It was unlikely Hanson knew the other man was marrying on the day Hanson murdered him, Mary being unscheduled collateral.

In Luke's mind, all Hanson really wanted was the contents of that carpetbag. Years worth of Hanson's dealings and illegal earnings. From experience, Luke knew giving him the files would not appease Hanson. He wasn't stupid enough to leave witnesses behind.

Not that Luke had any intention of handing over the precious evidence. It was almost as important to him as Mary had turned out to be.

Luke was becoming frustrated with Hanson. The outlaw on the other side of the door obviously didn't care how long it took. He seemed quite happy to wait. Luke, on the other hand, would rather they got it over and done with.

He would put a bullet in Hanson, and anyone with him before he would see Mary harmed.

Suddenly, everything changed. A bevy of bullets came through the door, and shattered the window on the other side of the room.

Mary screamed, much to Luke's horror, because now Hanson knew Mary was there with him.

"Over here!" a voice called from behind him. Luke spun to face the windows and discovered Peter.

"What…? How…?" He was totally confused. Luke hurried to the window and saw Peter was standing on a ladder. There were two men below him, on the ground. Luke recognized one as another marshal. Everything began to fall into place.

The task he'd assigned Peter was to organize help. Luke knew once Hanson located them, he would need additional men.

"Get Mary out here," Peter demanded, and Luke knew he was right.

"Be careful. Bullets are coming through the door," Luke said, then hurried into the closet to get Mary. He also snatched up the carpetbag.

"Hurry," he told Mary. "We want you to get out of this alive."

She stared at Peter and the ladder. Mary shook her head, but said nothing. "Hurry," Peter said. "There's no time to waste."

She was frozen to the spot, and Luke had to hold her close to convince her to go without him. "I'll be right behind you, I promise," he said. "Peter will help you down the ladder. You won't be alone."

It was clear Mary wasn't convinced, and Luke wasn't sure how to get around her stubbornness. Suddenly, another bullet came through the door and barely missed her. She no longer needed convincing.

He watched as Mary descended the ladder, and eventually reached solid ground. He climbed over the edge to the ladder and reached for the carpetbag he and Peter had destroyed. Another bullet came rushing in, far too close for comfort. It was clear Hanson was spraying bullets haphazardly, and any one of them could be fatal.

As he carefully climbed down the ladder, all the time juggling the bag, Peter called for him to toss it down. It was the last thing Luke wanted to do, for fear the contents would spray out everywhere.

Luke continued, and soon reached the ground and Mary.

The moment his feet touched solid ground, Mary ran to him, circling him with her arms. He didn't hesitate to pull her close, and at that moment decided he never wanted to let her go.

Chapter Twenty-One

Mary sobbed as she stood in Luke's arms.

The day Donald was killed, she was understandably upset, but today, when she believed she would lose Luke, Mary was certain her heart would stop. Their marriage might be a fake, but her feelings for him certainly were not.

They were more real than she'd ever felt for Donald. Mary finally understood her dead husband didn't love her. If anything, he was using her. To deflect his illegal activities, perhaps. She had been caught up in the romance of it all.

Being wooed by Donald McTavish was the best she'd ever been treated. If only Mary had seen his actions were superficial. He didn't love her, and Mary was certain he never had. Not once had he held her the way Luke did. Not once did he tell her he loved her, or that he needed her in his life.

Oh, he bought her lots of gifts—flowers, gowns, and dinner. Everything he thought would make her love him. But Mary never did. Until recently she believed she did, but she was foolish, and had no idea what true love was like.

Luke kissed her forehead, and pulled her a little closer. "Are you alright?" he asked.

She nodded despite shaking all over and feeling as though she might collapse at any moment. "Is…is Hanson still outside our room?" Mary asked in a small voice. She felt Luke's hand move across her back, and felt even more comforted than before.

"By now, he will be under arrest."

Mary was on the one hand relieved at Luke's words, but needed reassurance her ordeal really was over.

"I went to see the sheriff," Peter said, "and coincidentally, he had some marshals there for another crime they were investigating. I saw them take two men toward the jail a short time ago. I believe Hanson was one of them."

Luke pulled a folded piece of paper from his jacket. "Was this man one of them?" he asked, showing the picture to Peter, not for the first time.

"It certainly looks like him," Peter said.

Mary breathed a sigh of relief, and then the entire world went black.

"…not surprised." Mary heard the muffled voices and glanced about. She didn't recognize the room she was in, and sat up abruptly. Her heart pounded. Panic began to set in, and she was hyperventilating.

The last time she'd done that, it had caused her to be even more lightheaded. Mary tried to slow her breathing.

"Ah, you're awake," an unfamiliar voice said.

Mary spun around, causing even more dizziness. A hand covered hers, and she glanced up to see Luke standing next to her. "You're safe," he told her. "This is Doctor Jones. He has been taking care of you after you fainted."

"Fainted?" Mary didn't recall fainting, but if Luke said so, she must have.

"It's the shock," Doctor Jones told her. "I understand a lot has happened over the past couple of weeks. Having people shoot at you would certainly cause you to go into shock." He held her wrist, and Mary assumed the doctor was checking her heart rate. "Better," he said, then got up close to her face and looked into Mary's eyes. "Good. Do you feel like getting up?"

She glanced at Luke, who was still by her side. "I'm here for you," he told her, and Mary wished that could be true.

Luke held her hand and helped Mary to sit up. Slight dizziness occurred, but she was determined to stand on her own two feet. His hands around her waist, Mary glanced at him. There were stress lines around his eyes. She hadn't noticed them before. Since the outlaw was now in jail, she thought he would be more relaxed.

"We'll do this slowly," Luke said, helping her to the floor. Instead of dropping his hands as Mary thought he would, Luke held her tightly. He stared into her face, his expression softening.

"I…I need fresh air," she whispered.

Luke looked to the doctor who nodded his approval. His hands stayed on her waist as the pair went outside. The wooden bench outside the doctor's office was not particularly comfortable, but Mary was grateful for somewhere to sit.

"Finally," Luke said when they were alone, "your ordeal is over. What are you going to do now?"

Her heart pounded so loudly, it sounded as though a train was approaching them. She shook her head in disbelief. Was Luke ready to let her go? To arrange their annulment? Tears filled her eyes, and she turned her head away. She didn't want Luke to see how weak she had become.

"Mary? Tell me what you're thinking," he demanded without raising his voice.

She spun around to face him, despite the hot tears running down her face. "I'm in love with you, Luke," she said, brushing the tears from her cheeks.

Mary's fake husband stared at her for what seemed an eternity. His thumbs brushed at her face, wiping away the tears that refused to stop. Then he pulled her close and wrapped his arms around her. "I don't want an annulment," he said, his voice emotional. "I am in love with you, Mary. In the beginning, I believed it was because we were forced together. Except I've come to realize it is pure love. I could never live without you."

He pushed Mary away from himself and put his hands to her face, then moved in closer. Luke stared into her eyes, watching her, and not saying a word.

"Oh, for goodness sake," Mary said. "Just kiss me." And that's exactly what he did.

~*~

Since they were already married, there was no wedding ceremony to be held. Instead, they held a small celebration at her parent's property with their closest friends, including Peter Jameson.

Luke's superiors were not impressed with his resignation, but they understood. It seemed to Mary it wasn't the first time they'd lost marshals to love.

Mary didn't want to return to Douglas McTavish's home—there were far too many bad memories associated with it. After the marshals had finished looking for evidence, Luke helped her remove all her personal items. Instead of selling Douglas's home, which she inherited, Mary donated it to the church, who gladly accepted the gift. Many children would be housed in what would become an orphanage.

Instead, the pair went to live in the farmhouse Mary had inherited from her parents. The farm wasn't huge, but it was enough for them to keep busy and make a small stipend to keep them happy.

Both Luke and Mary knew it would be a wonderful place to bring up children, should they be blessed in that way.

Epilogue

Two years later…

Luke and Mary sat on the porch, staring out over their property. It had grown substantially since they began to work the land. For Luke, it was a massive change to his previous life, but he wasn't complaining. "I will never tire of how peaceful it is out here," Luke said, reaching for Mary's hand. "The only regret I have is the circumstance under which we met. I know it was incredibly stressful for you."

Mary stared at him momentarily. "It was stressful," she said quietly. "My only regret is that my parents never got to meet you. I know they would have loved you as much as I do."

Luke leaned in then and stole a kiss. His hand went to his wife's swollen belly. It wouldn't be long, and baby number two would arrive. Their young son, Peter Lucas, was sound asleep. The boy still needed his nap time, even if he did protest.

"I wonder what Peter's reaction will be when the baby arrives," Mary said, and Luke couldn't help but chuckle.

"It could be interesting," Luke replied. "Any more babies and I'll have to extend the farmhouse," he said. "This place was never built for a big family."

Mary stared at him. "Are you complaining?" she asked.

He held his hand to her belly and felt their unborn baby kick. "Not at all," he told her. "This farm is the perfect place to bring up children. I'm certain you would agree since you grew up here."

Mary's face pinched, and Luke knew exactly what was going on. "Time for the doc?" he asked as he stood. Luke helped Mary to her feet, and began to walk her inside.

"It's a bit early," Mary said, waving his concerns aside. "Oh my goodness!" she suddenly declared, as her waters broke. "Perhaps you are right after all."

He finished walking his wife inside, and helped her into the bed. "I'll arrange the doc," he said once she was settled and comfortable. He would get one of the farmhands to ride into town and fetch Doc Miller.

Luke knew they were in for a long day, as babies did like to take their time. After arranging for someone to get the doctor, he sat back down on the front porch for only a moment. His time was spent praying for the safe delivery of their baby, and for

Mary's well-being. He loved her more than life itself.

~*~

With young Peter in his arms, Luke anxiously paced outside as he awaited the birth of their second child. Doc Miller had been with Mary for some hours. It wasn't unusual he knew, but this birth was definitely taking longer than their son's.

It was concerning, but each time Luke tried to enter the farmhouse, he was turned away. "I'll let you know the moment the baby is born," the nurse told him. "It shouldn't be long now."

She smiled at him, but the last thing Luke wanted to do was smile. What if he lost Mary? His heart sank—Luke didn't even want to contemplate that possibility. He sat on the porch with young Peter, holding the boy close to his heart. Eventually, Peter fell asleep in his arms.

Luke's foreman climbed the front steps. "Any word yet?" he asked. All the farmhands adored Mary. She treated everyone with kindness, even after everything she'd endured.

"Not a thing," Luke told him. "Hopefully it won't be much longer." He sat back on the porch chair as he patted Peter's back. "Wait," he said. "Did you hear that?" He looked eagerly at his foreman. "It sounded like a baby crying."

Luke slowly stood. Had his prayers been answered? His heart thudded as he stepped toward the front door. He peered through the front window, trying to see inside. Suddenly, the door opened.

"Congratulations, Luke," the nurse told him. "It's a girl," she said, then a tiny smile crossed her lips. "And a boy."

Luke stared at her, but said not a word.

"Twins, Luke," she said firmly. "Your wife delivered two babies. All three are healthy, but Mary is exhausted as you can imagine. I'll let you know when you can visit with her." The nurse spun around and left him standing there, his mouth gaping.

Luke faced his foreman. "Did I hear that correctly?" he said, still in disbelief. "Twins?"

"You sure did," the foreman told him. "Life is going to get interesting now."

Luke knew he was right. It was only moments later when he was called inside to see his wife. Mary was propped up in the bed, a baby in each arm. "Mary," he whispered, still trying to take in the news. "This is a surprise." He leaned in and kissed her forehead. "I love you so much," Luke said as he dropped to his knees next to the bed.

Mary smiled, then chuckled. "Remember how we picked out two names—one for a boy, and another for a girl? There's no longer a problem," she said, and Luke knew she was right.

When he was sent to talk with Douglas McTavish, little did he know it would end with him marrying the criminal's new wife. It may have started with a fake marriage, but her real husband was even more in love with his wife than ever.

His prayers had been answered, even though back then, a real marriage was not the outcome he'd predicted. Luke knew God had a plan for him, but until he met Mary, he had no idea what it was.

He was grateful for every moment they were together, and knew they would be together for all eternity.

From the Author

Thank you so much for reading my book – I hope you enjoyed it.

I would greatly appreciate you leaving a review where you purchased, even if it is only a one-liner. It helps to have my books more visible!

About the Author

Multi-published, award-winning and bestselling author Cheryl Wright, former secretary, debt collector, account manager, writing coach, and shopping tour hostess, loves reading.

She writes both historical and contemporary western romance, as well as romantic suspense.

She lives in Melbourne, Australia, and is married with two adult children and has six grandchildren, and twin great-grandchildren.

When she's not writing, she can be found in her craft room making greeting cards.

Links

Website: *http://www.cheryl-wright.com/*

Facebook Reader Group:
https://www.facebook.com/groups/cherylwrightauthor/

Join My Newsletter:

https://cheryl-wright.com/newsletter/
(and receive a free book)

www.ingramcontent.com/pod-product-compliance
Lightning Source LLC
Chambersburg PA
CBHW072146130726
47909CB00004BB/1247